PUFFIN BOOKS

Maybe

Morris Gleitzman grew up in England and went to live in
Australia when he was sixteen. He worked as a frozen-chicken
thawer, sugar-mill rolling-stock unhooker, fashion-industry
trainee, department-store Santa, TV producer, newspaper
columnist and screenwriter. Then he had a wonderful experience.
He wrote a novel for young people. Now he's one of
the bestselling children's authors in Australia. He lives in
Brisbane and Sydney and visits Britain regularly. His many books
include *Two Weeks with the Queen*, *Bumface*,
Boy Overboard and *Once*.

Visit Morris at his website:
morrisgleitzman.com

C334149997

Also by Morris Gleitzman

Maybe

MORRIS GLEITZMAN

PUFFIN

PUFFIN BOOKS

UK | USA | Canada | Ireland | Australia
India | New Zealand | South Africa

Puffin Books is part of the Penguin Random House group of companies
whose addresses can be found at global.penguinrandomhouse.com.

www.penguin.co.uk
www.puffin.co.uk
www.ladybird.co.uk

Penguin
Random House
UK

First published by Penguin Random House Australia Pty Ltd
and in Great Britain by Puffin Books 2017

001

Design by Tony Palmer
Set in 13/15pt Minion by Penguin Random House Australia Pty Ltd
Printed in Great Britain by Clays Ltd, St Ives plc

ISBN: 978–0–141–38865–6

For all the children
who dreamed of a safe place.

And for all the countries
who offered one.

Maybe it won't happen.

Maybe everything will be fine.

Maybe I should just stop thinking about the bad things and concentrate on the good things.

Like this beautiful countryside we're walking through. Birds chirping and butterflies fluttering and not a single one of them being blown up.

And this dust on the road. It's very good dust. Soft under our boots. Cushioning our cartwheels. Which is the best thing you could wish for when you've got a pregnant person in your cart. And another person walking next to you who's nearly forty years old with sore feet.

My favourite thing of all is this warm and fragrant spring breeze. In all the years I've been alive, 1946 is definitely the best year for fragrant breezes. I think it's because there aren't so many dead bodies around.

For now.

'Felix,' says Gabriek, 'are your legs hurting?'

Even with my dusty glasses I can see Gabriek's concerned look. He knows my legs give me trouble sometimes and we've been walking for days.

'They're fine, thanks,' I say.

Actually, they are a bit sore. But I bet Gabriek's are too, and Henk the donkey's, so I'm not going to complain about mine.

'Good,' says Gabriek. 'In that case, stop frowning and cheer up.'

I give him an indignant look.

Can't he see how much effort I'm putting into not frowning?

'Lighten up, Felix,' says Anya from the cart. 'You've got a face like a Nazi's bum.'

I give her an indignant look too. I open my mouth to tell them both about the fragrant breezes and the soft dust. But for some reason the words get stuck and won't come out.

'You're doing it again, aren't you?' says Gabriek. 'Thinking about a certain person.'

I shake my head. I point to a butterfly.

'Felix,' says Gabriek quietly. 'We agreed not to think about him.'

Gabriek's right. We did.

'I'm trying not to,' I say. 'It's hard.'

'I know,' says Gabriek. 'But he'll never find us. Never. Not where we're going.'

'That's right,' says Anya. 'Zliv doesn't have a clue about Gabriek's farm. Nobody in the city does.

Even I didn't before you told me, and you know how nosy I am.'

'So,' Gabriek says to me, 'no more frowning and worrying. Promise?'

I give Gabriek another look. He's a dear and caring friend, but he's treating me like a six-year-old. Which you shouldn't do to someone who's fourteen and who knows how many things in the world need worrying about.

'Come on, Felix,' says Anya. 'We all have to make an effort. The butterflies are, you can too.'

I give Anya another look. I love having her in our family. And I'm very grateful to her for a lot of things. But sometimes she forgets she's only a couple of years older than me. Oh well, she'll have to stop treating me like a kid if everything goes bad and I end up delivering her baby.

I feel my face getting hot and I look away.

I shouldn't be thinking about things like that. Not yet. I haven't even finished reading the baby book.

'We made a deal,' says Gabriek. 'We've all spent too many years looking over our shoulders for murdering thugs. Specially you, Felix. So we're coming here for a life without fear. Right?'

I nod.

'Good,' says Gabriek.

But I'm still anxious.

I've been trying the whole journey not to be, but I can't help it.

You know how when you live in a violent city after a war and a murdering thug called Gogol gets killed so you think life will be safer and happier but then you hear that Gogol's brother Zliv has come back from Croatia where he was killing people for money and he blames you for his brother's death and he's telling everyone that he won't rest till he's cut your heart out and so you and Anya and Gabriek head off in secret to live on Gabriek's farm but for most of the journey you worry that the farm isn't far enough away plus you start wishing you hadn't swapped your medical books for a donkey?

That's happening to me.

'Almost there,' says Gabriek. 'Less than an hour.'

He gives the reins a tug.

Behind us Henk the donkey plods faster. The cart rattles and squeaks even more than it has for the last nineteen days.

I make an even bigger effort to concentrate on the good things. To forget what everyone in the city says about Zliv. That he's an even more ruthless killer than his brother. That when he decides you should die, he never gives up.

Ever.

I take the reins from Gabriek.

'My turn,' I say.

I give the reins another tug. We need to get to the farm as soon as possible and start our peaceful new life.

Last year, before the war ended, the Nazis burned

Gabriek's farmhouse down, so we've got a lot of rebuilding to do.

The local midwife probably won't come and deliver Anya's baby without a proper farmhouse with a proper roof. And a kitchen with a stove so if the midwife hears the baby's father is a dead Russian soldier and she gets disgusted and tries to leave, we can stop her with hot tea and cakes.

Henk isn't going any faster. I whistle at him and give his reins a harder tug.

He still doesn't speed up.

He goes slower. Much slower.

And stops.

We all go tense. We know what this means.

Donkeys have very good hearing. Henk always hears trucks before we do.

'Take cover,' mutters Gabriek.

Now we can all hear the truck in the distance. We know the routine. When you've been on the road this long you learn lots of things, including that trucks are sometimes driven by vicious bandits and criminal deserters.

Or worse.

Gabriek grabs Henk's reins and steers the cart off the road into the trees.

I jump onto the cart to help Anya.

'Sorry about before,' she says. 'You're right, there are some things we have to worry about.'

We look at each other, then I help her pull a blanket over herself.

Another thing we've learned on the road is how lots of people have the wrong idea about pregnant women. They think pregnant women are weak and easy to rob.

Those people don't know Anya.

From under the blanket I hear a familiar sound. The safety catch being released on a gun.

Gabriek stops the cart behind some bushes. I jump down and crouch next to him. We peer through the bushes at the road.

The truck sounds close.

Please, I say silently. Let it just be vicious bandits or criminal deserters.

There's a loud buzzing. A large horsefly is hovering near my face. I brush it away. It lands on Henk's neck, on a patch where the fur is very short.

I realise what I've done.

Don't, I beg silently. Don't sting Henk.

It does.

Henk gives a scream and starts to bolt.

The reins are torn out of Gabriek's hands. I grab them as they slither past, which jerks me forward and my glasses are torn off and I'm dragged through the undergrowth. Twigs stab me and creepers whip me. I should have just let the horsefly sting me.

'Henk,' I hear a voice yell. 'Stop.'

It's not Gabriek's voice, it's Anya's.

We seem to be slowing down a bit. I can see a blurry tree stump looming towards me. I roll to one side and hook my legs round the stump and clamp them tight. My arm and leg sockets stretch painfully, but I don't let go of the reins.

We stop.

'Good boy, Henk,' says Anya.

I look up, squinting.

Anya is on Henk's back, her big tummy against his neck. She must have jumped onto him.

'Anya,' I say. 'You shouldn't . . .'

Gabriek drags me to my feet and pushes my glasses into my hands.

'Quick,' he says. 'All of us. Out of sight.'

Too late. I put my glasses on just in time to see the truck on the road. As it passes, it slows down. We're out in the open. The faces peering from the cab can see us clearly.

'Poop,' mutters Anya. 'My gun's in the cart.'

We stand frozen.

I stare at the faces in the truck. A man and a woman, both younger than Gabriek.

Just like Zliv.

The man is wearing a military uniform. The woman isn't. They both stare at us.

The truck slows down and stops.

'It's not him,' mutters Gabriek, giving my shoulder a squeeze.

He's telling me not to run. Running always makes you look guilty. Soldiers shoot when you run.

The man and the woman get out of the truck.

I peer around for a weapon to use.

We can't be sure it's not Zliv. We've never even seen him. Anyone can steal an army truck. And if a woman's hungry enough she'll probably travel with a ruthless killer for as long as he wants.

I remember another story I heard about Zliv. About a girlfriend he had in Croatia. One day she joked about how Zliv was much skinnier than his brother. Zliv got angry. And made her skinny too. With a knife.

'I'm getting my gun,' mutters Anya.

'Don't,' hisses Gabriek.

The woman is coming towards us. The man is behind her, hurrying to keep up.

For a second I think the woman is trying to get away from him. Then I see what she's doing.

Staring directly at me. With a strange expression. As if she recognises me. As if she knows me.

Which is weird because I don't think I've ever seen her before. Was she a nun in the orphanage I hid in ages ago? Or one of the partisan freedom fighters I lived with in the forest?

I don't think so.

The woman is close now.

She suddenly stops. Her face collapses with disappointment. She makes sorry movements with her hands and turns away, hurrying past the man back towards the truck.

The man hesitates, looking at us.

He's not Zliv. A ruthless killer wouldn't have such a concerned expression.

'Mistake,' says the man. 'She thought . . . sorry, my Polish is bad.'

His uniform looks sort of English.

'I speak English,' I say.

Which is a slight exaggeration. I've been learning it, but I haven't used it much in dangerous military situations.

The man looks at me, surprised. He switches to English, but with an unusual accent.

'My friend got confused,' he says. 'She thought you were someone she'd looked after in hospital. Sorry to give you a fright. Bye.'

By the time I've worked out what the words mean, the man has turned and is heading back to the truck. The woman is already inside. The man gets in and they drive away.

I realise I'm trembling. My muscles are aching. That happens when they've been getting ready to run. Or fight.

I look at Gabriek and Anya. I can see they're feeling the same.

'Lucky escape,' says Gabriek.

'For them,' says Anya.

She's holding her gun.

I agree with Gabriek. It was a lucky escape. It wasn't Zliv this time, but it could have been. And even with Anya's gun, if he'd driven at us fast in the truck, with a machine gun out the window . . .

Gabriek is looking at me.

He can probably see who I'm thinking about.

'Gabriek,' I say. 'I think we need to make a new plan for our future life.'

I didn't know I was going to say that. It just came out. But now I've said it, I mean it.

'New plan?' says Gabriek. 'What sort of new plan?'

'It's me that Zliv's after,' I say. 'So it'll be safer if I live separately. I'll find a place somewhere in the district. So at least if Zliv finds me, you and Anya won't be there.'

I can see Gabriek doesn't like the idea. And the way Anya's glaring at me, she doesn't either.

I don't like it much myself.

It's making me feel sick.

But it's for the best.

'We can still see each other,' I say. 'We can have secret meetings in the forest. Several times a week if we like.'

My voice is wobbling, which isn't the best way to persuade people about an unpleasant but necessary new plan.

'Felix,' mutters Anya. 'Stop it.'

Gabriek just looks at me.

I can see how moved he is. And how annoyed.

When he finally speaks, his voice doesn't wobble at all.

'You're a remarkable person, Felix,' he says. 'Brave and generous. But you're forgetting a couple of things. It was Anya who blew up Gogol's truck and me who killed him.'

'Exactly,' says Anya. 'So Zliv wants our guts just as much as he wants yours, Felix.'

'No, he doesn't,' I say. 'You heard what people were saying in the city. Zliv blames me for his brother's death. Rants and yells about how if I hadn't poked my nose in, Gogol would still be alive today.'

Gabriek closes his eyes.

When he does that, apart from at bedtime, it's usually because he's heard something he disagrees with so much that his cardiovascular system and digestive tract are hurting.

'It's for the best,' I stammer.

Gabriek opens his eyes and looks at me.

'We're in this together,' he says.

I want to argue.

I want to tell him that being in it together means trying to keep each other safe. Giving each other good protection.

Even if that means not actually being together.

But I don't. The expression on Gabriek's face tells me it would be a waste of time.

Gabriek gives my shoulder another squeeze.

'Come on,' he says. 'Let's get to the farm.'

Maybe Gabriek has forgotten.

Maybe he doesn't remember how sometimes you have to leave someone to protect them.

Which is what Mum and Dad did for me.

I won't ever forget them. I keep my memory strong by learning new words and new knowledge. I have to do it every day. Your memory isn't always the best when you've had lots of explosions in your childhood and not enough vitamins.

My memory is working well today, judging by how much I'm recognising things around us.

I haven't seen this countryside for over a year and last time it was covered in frost and Nazis so it looked a bit different.

But I still recognise it.

Gabriek does too. He's so excited at the thought of seeing his farm again, he's almost running. The cart is jolting and squeaking. Henk's legs are moving faster than they have the whole journey.

So are mine.

'Hey,' yells Anya from the cart. 'Go easy.'

'Sorry,' says Gabriek.

He slows Henk down.

I don't blame Anya for being annoyed. If I'd been pregnant every day for the last seven and a half months, I'd probably be feeling grumpy too.

And anxious.

Anya is amazing. She doesn't seem anxious at all about Zliv or about the baby arriving in only six weeks. And she knows it's going to be a tough job, rebuilding Gabriek's farmhouse in that amount of time. I told her how when I last saw the place, it was just a pile of smoking rubble.

But a tough job is good. It keeps you occupied. Stops you worrying about things you're not meant to be worrying about.

To stop myself worrying now, I look at Anya.

She's curled up on her blanket in the back of the cart, reading the baby book. She's nearly finished it, which is also good.

Amazing actually.

Because I can remember exactly how she carried on the first time she saw it.

'That's crazy,' said Anya when I gave her the baby book a few months ago. 'It's in English. You've got a whole ex-Nazi medical library piled up in your room, there must be a baby book in Polish.'

I shook my head.

'The Nazis didn't like Polish books,' I said. 'And I don't like Nazi ones. Specially Nazi baby books. They're full of unkind instructions about which babies should live and which ones shouldn't.'

Anya didn't argue with that.

'Here's a suggestion,' said Gabriek. 'Why don't you both learn English? Then you'll understand every word.'

We stared at him.

'Learn English?' said Anya.

'You know a bit already,' said Gabriek to Anya. 'From all those British and American soldiers you used to sell things to. You know some as well, Felix. From when we had our mending business and we branched out into soldiers' boots.'

Anya snorted.

'I speak about ten words,' she said.

'After a war,' said Gabriek, 'smart people learn the language of the side that won.'

Me and Anya thought about this.

It made sense.

And now here's Anya, reading happily in the back of the cart, not even fussed by difficult English words like cervix and placenta.

Anya looks up from the baby book and sees me watching her.

She gives me a smile.

I wish she wouldn't do that. I might have to be her doctor in a few weeks and the feeling I get when she smiles at me like that isn't the sort of feeling a doctor should have with a patient.

I give her a quick smile back and turn away. My face is hot again. And not just because I'm walking fast to keep up with Gabriek. To calm myself down I wipe my glasses and peer into the distance.

Up ahead is a hill covered in trees.

A very familiar hill.

We must be almost there. I feel myself relaxing. I start feeling happy and hopeful about all the good things waiting for us in the future.

That happens when Anya smiles at me.

We reach the top of the hill.

Gabriek steers Henk and the cart off the road and into the trees. After he tethers Henk, he peers down the other side of the hill.

I do too. I recognise the hillside. And the small road winding down it. Leading to something else I recognise.

The gate to Gabriek's farm.

I stare.

This isn't what I expected.

I look at Gabriek. I can see it isn't what he expected either.

I thought there'd be abandoned fields and in the middle of them a pile of rubble that used to be the farmhouse.

But the fields aren't abandoned. They've got cabbages and turnips growing in them.

And the rubble is gone. The farmyard is a patch of clean raw dirt.

There are men in the farmyard, quite a few of them. I see what the men are doing.

Rebuilding the farmhouse.

My insides tingle with excitement.

I peer down through the trees at the big pieces of timber the men are lifting and the careful way they're hammering them to make a roof frame.

Friendly neighbours helping to rebuild things after the war.

Me and Gabriek did that in the city. Helped our neighbours mend their places. Lots of people did. Nobody asked for money. Just a bit of pork fat or a few English lessons.

'Gabriek,' says Anya, climbing out of the cart. 'What are those people doing on your farm?'

Anya hasn't had much experience with friendly neighbours. Before she lived with Gabriek and me, most of the people she met weren't friendly at all. Including the man who made her pregnant.

'If we're lucky,' says Gabriek, squinting down the hill, 'that lot are building me a new house.'

'Let's find out,' says Anya.

She grabs her pistol and clicks the safety catch off.

Gabriek puts his hand on the gun.

'I need you to stay here, Anya,' he says. 'Out of sight. To protect our belongings.'

Anya opens her mouth to protest.

Gabriek gives her a look.

She scowls but doesn't say anything. Gabriek is the kindest friend in the world, but he's stubborn. Specially about good protection. So you don't argue.

Anya offers her gun to me.

It's a kind thought, but I won't need it. And I'm hoping that after Anya watches me and Gabriek go down the hill to greet the men, she'll start to feel she can meet neighbours without a gun too.

'No thanks,' I say to her. 'It's better if we look friendly.'

I turn to Gabriek, who must be as excited about all this as I am.

But he isn't looking excited at all.

He's staring at the distant men, frowning.

When Gabriek frowns, there's usually a good reason.

I realise with a sick feeling what it probably is. Something we've both experienced quite a lot. Something I shouldn't ever forget.

After a war has happened, things can sometimes look good when they're actually very bad.

Maybe worrying is a habit you can catch. Maybe Gabriek's caught it from me.

But maybe he's wrong and those men down there are just friendly neighbours.

We'll soon find out.

'Can we slow down a bit?' I say to Gabriek.

He's so caught up in his thoughts as we hurry down the hillside, he hasn't noticed I'm in pain. And my limp is getting worse. Which can happen when you use bad legs to stop a bolting donkey.

'Sorry,' says Gabriek.

We slow down a bit.

The closer we get to the farm, the better I feel. Partly because of the memories I'm having.

I spent two of the happiest years of my life on this farm.

OK, it was mostly in a hole under the barn, but you can be very happy in a hole if you've got someone like Gabriek looking after you.

There were sad things too, very sad things, but when you spend a lot of time alone you learn to concentrate on the good things. Like the food Gabriek brought me. The stories we told each other. The very useful things he taught me for my education. The good protection he gave me.

I was very lucky.

Gabriek glances back up the hill towards where Anya is hiding among the trees.

'Let's keep it relaxed and friendly,' he says.

I know what he's thinking. If things do get difficult, Anya won't be able to stop herself. She'll come rushing to help. And I'm almost certain the baby book would advise against a person in her condition running down a hill waving a gun.

'She's pretty incredible, isn't she?' says Gabriek. 'Everything she's been through.'

I nod.

I think she's very incredible.

Gabriek looks at me. For a bit too long. I feel myself starting to blush.

I change the subject.

'Very well-cut timber,' I say.

I point to the men in the farmyard and the good job they're doing. Well-cut timber, carefully positioned and thoughtfully joined. They're obviously people who take pride in their work. Who want to contribute to their community.

Gabriek always says that to build something well you need a good heart.

We speed up again, which is OK. I'm looking forward to meeting our good neighbours.

We'll compliment them on their work and thank them for their generosity. Tell them that when Gabriek's farmhouse is finished, we'll help them build anything else that's needed. Schools, hospitals, chicken sheds, we're very experienced builders.

And of course I'll tell them I'm happy to share my medical experience with the whole community.

'Here we go,' says Gabriek.

The men have seen us.

I wave to them as we go in through the farm gate. They don't wave back. They've all stopped working and they're standing with their hands on their hips, staring at us.

Which is normal after a war.

'So,' says Gabriek loudly to the men. 'Bit of a surprise, this.'

That didn't really sound as friendly as I think he meant it to.

'A good surprise,' I say to the men.

The men's expressions don't change. They keep staring in a not very friendly way.

'I wonder,' says Gabriek to the men, still loudly, 'how should I feel about this?'

The men don't seem to know.

'Delighted?' says Gabriek. 'Or not so delighted?'

One of the men, glaring down from a roof beam, spits onto the ground at Gabriek's feet.

'You should feel scared,' says the man. 'Terrified. Wetting your pants.'

Gabriek looks at the man for several moments. I can hear somebody's heart beating loudly and I think it's mine.

'And why should I be scared on my own farm?' says Gabriek.

Several of the other men take steps towards us.

Gabriek doesn't move, so I don't.

'Because it's not your farm any more,' says the man on the beam.

I'm shocked.

But Gabriek stays calm. He doesn't say anything.

'We didn't think you'd be stupid enough to come back here, Borowski,' says another man. 'Not after what you did.'

Gabriek looks at the man.

'And what was that, Mr Placek?' he says, starting to sound annoyed.

'Hiding vermin,' says the man. 'Putting the whole district at risk. All our families.'

The men are looking at me now.

I feel sick.

I want to yell at them, 'The war's over. The Nazis are defeated. Why are you doing this?'

But Gabriek said we should be relaxed and friendly. I think I know why.

These men might be finding it hard after six years of war to get used to it being over. Specially if some of their loved ones were killed.

I know how that feels.

So it's best for us all to be extra friendly.

I open my mouth to tell the men what good builders they are and to ask them if they've got any hospitals me and Gabriek can help with.

Before I can say it, Gabriek speaks again.

'Hiding vermin?' he says. 'I don't know what you're talking about.'

The man up on the roof beam snaps his fingers.

Another man goes over to a rubbish heap and rummages among old bits of wood and charred bricks and empty food tins and what looks like a couple of dead rats.

He comes over to me and Gabriek, smoothing out several screwed-up pieces of paper that are burnt at the edges.

I stare at them.

I thought I'd never see them again.

Zelda's drawings. And a story I wrote about the good protection I got on this farm. I left them all in my hole for people to find after the war was over. So they'd know. But when the Nazis burned the barn down, I thought my evidence got destroyed too.

The men are still glaring at me.

As if they hate me.

Maybe hating is another habit people catch.

A difficult one to give up, by the looks of it. If my best friend's funny drawings and my own grateful story haven't cheered these men up, I don't think anything will.

I stare unhappily at the pieces of paper again. My evidence has turned into evidence against me. I don't know whether to feel grateful the pages have survived, or not so grateful.

Yes I do.

I snatch the pages so fast the man who was holding them looks dazed. But only for a moment. Then he moves towards me.

Gabriek moves towards him.

'Get off my farm,' says Gabriek.

'You didn't hear us,' says the man on the beam. 'It's not your farm any more. You forfeited it when you let that Jew vermin pollute the place.'

The veins in Gabriek's throat go tight.

Medically, that can be a dangerous thing.

For the men as well.

'So,' says the man on the beam to Gabriek. 'You get off my farm.'

Gabriek doesn't say anything for quite a while.

Just stands very still, thinking.

I wonder if he's thinking what I'm thinking. How chances are, none of these men were partisan fighters. So none of them have had any weapons training. So if they attack us, me and Gabriek are probably the only ones here who know how to kill quickly with blunt pieces of wood.

Probably best if Gabriek isn't thinking that. The moment one of us grabs an offcut, Anya will be hurling herself down the hillside, risking her life and the baby's.

Gabriek gives the men a big smile.

'I'm thinking this is a matter for the town hall,' he says. 'What do you say? Shall we all go into town?'

The men look confused.

They glance at each other, frowning.

I'm a bit confused too.

Then the man on the beam laughs. It's not a friendly laugh.

'Yes,' he says. 'Let's.'

He gives a look to one of the other men, who gets on a rusty old motorbike and starts the engine.

For a second I think he's going to give me and Gabriek a lift, but he roars off on his own.

'Good,' says Gabriek, still smiling at the men.

Suddenly, to their amazement and mine too, Gabriek starts shaking all the men by the hand.

The men are so stunned, they let him.

Incredible. Is Gabriek taking a gamble that, deep down, everyone wants to live in peace?

No, I think he's just being very smart.

Up the hill, Anya will be watching this. When she sees everyone being so friendly, she'll probably decide not to come down here with her gun.

Not yet, anyway.

I don't know why the men made us wait for this horse and cart.

The town's not that far away. We could have walked faster than this poor half-dead horse and this rickety old cart that smells of pigs.

And we wouldn't be sharing the journey with three of the nastiest people I've ever met.

I try to ignore them and the looks of hatred they keep giving me. Which isn't easy when we're all sitting knee to knee.

'Jew vermin,' mutters one of the men under his breath.

I feel Gabriek go tense next to me. I try to show him he doesn't have to get stressed or violent.

'If you think you're hurting my feelings,' I say to the man, 'you're not. I know you're just trying to make trouble because you want Gabriek's farm.'

Gabriek smiles grimly.

'Very perceptive, Felix,' he says, not taking his eyes off the three men. 'Isn't that right, Placek? You always were a greedy little sulk, even at school. And you, Milowski, you were stealing things even then, weren't you? And Szynsky, wasn't it you who used to torture cats?'

The men don't say anything, just scowl.

This time I don't try to make things friendly. I scowl back at the men. Anya can't see us now and these men deserve it.

Mr Szynsky smirks, possibly at the memory of the cats.

'You don't get it, do you?' he says to Gabriek.

'Oh, I get it,' says Gabriek. 'I get that things have changed. The bad days are over. So you'd better get ready for some decency and justice.'

The men don't look convinced.

I'm tempted to tell them they won't be ready till they get the hatred out of their hearts. But I don't bother. They wouldn't hear me now because we've reached the town and the cartwheels are very noisy on the cobblestones.

Years ago the Nazis got rid of the town council. There must be a new one that Gabriek's heard about, one that's already busy with decency and justice.

'By the way,' says Gabriek to the men. 'Who's the mayor these days?'

Mr Szynsky smirks even more than when he was thinking about the cats.

'I am,' he says.

For the first time in ages I see a flicker of fear on Gabriek's face.

Straight away he hides it.

I wish I was good at doing that. But I'm not. Specially not now. Because the cart is rumbling into the town square and I can see who's waiting for us.

Glaring at us.

Muttering and clenching their fists.

A large mob.

Maybe this isn't a mob.

Maybe all these people are just citizens having a meeting. Maybe they're angry because the town council hasn't been doing enough repairs.

Those big posts over there, for example. They look like they need attention. They're leaning badly and they're extremely weatherbeaten.

Oh.

I stare at the posts, feeling sick.

I think I recognise them.

They're bringing back memories I don't want to have. Please let these be different posts. Ones I've never seen before. Posts for holding up Christmas decorations or showing the prices of pigs in the market.

But they're not.

They're the ones.

I glance at Gabriek. I can tell from his face that he knows it too.

They're the posts the Nazis hanged people from.

Innocent, loving people who never did anything bad in their lives.

My best friend, Zelda.

Gabriek's wife, Genia.

I stare at the posts. Memories burn inside me.

Genia saving me from the Nazis. Zelda saving me from becoming a killer.

Me not able to save either of them.

Suddenly I'm grabbed by angry hands and pulled out of the cart and dragged across the cobblestones and now I know for certain that this is a mob.

'Stop,' I yell at them. 'You can't. The war is over. You can't do this any more.'

Nobody listens.

They yank me to my feet. I'm surrounded. Not just by men, by women and kids too. All shouting things and looking like they want to kill me.

I try to see Gabriek. But I can't. Just a seething mass of twisted faces.

'Gabriek,' I yell.

We have to stay close, watching each other's back like we always do.

And we must try to calm this mob. Offer them repairs to their town and medical attention and hot tea and cakes.

Except suddenly I don't want to do that. I want to get out of here. Go back to the city with Gabriek and Anya and take our chances with Zliv.

'So,' hisses a voice in my ear. 'The vermin returns.'

A familiar voice.

I haven't heard it for years.

But I know exactly who it is.

I turn. A boy is smirking at me, a boy of about my age with very fair hair and wet pink lips.

Cyryl Szynsky.

He sticks his face close to mine.

'I've missed you, Wilhelm,' says Cyryl. 'Where's your little friend?'

He sniggers and glances at the posts. He knows exactly what happened to Zelda.

I want to hurt him. But two men are holding my arms tightly and I can't.

'My name's not Wilhelm,' I say to him. 'It's Felix.'

No point using pretend names now. Four years ago, when I first met Cyryl, I needed to hide. Now I want them all to know the truth.

'Her name wasn't Violetta,' I say to Cyryl. 'It was Zelda. She was six, but she had the loving heart of a ten-year-old.'

Just saying her name makes me feel weak with sadness. I can see that Cyryl doesn't have a clue what a loving heart is.

'Big tough Cyryl,' I say to him. 'Betraying a little girl to the Nazis. Did it make you feel proud? Watching them kill her.'

Cyryl glances at the crowd around us who have gone quiet and are listening to this. He looks worried he might be in trouble. But nobody in the crowd tells him off because mobs don't care.

Most of this lot probably did similar things.

With a smirk, Cyryl puts his face close to mine again.

'What's the big deal about a dead Jew?' he says. 'Who cares if she was six or sixty? There's thousands of them in the forests around here. Good manure, that's what I say. And if you can be bothered digging them up, rich pickings.'

He holds his pudgy pink hand in front of my face. On his finger is a big gold ring with an eagle stamped on it.

'You have to pull the gold out of their vermin teeth,' says Cyryl. 'But it's worth it.'

All I can move is my neck.

I lunge forward, clamp my teeth round Cyryl's finger and bite with all my strength.

For Zelda. For Mum and Dad. For Genia and Barney and all the others.

The ring is inside my mouth. So is warm liquid, sticky and salty. My teeth grate against bone.

Cyryl is screaming.

The men holding me are shouting.

I keep biting. Until something hard smashes against my head. And again. Cyril drags his finger out of my mouth and I drop to the ground.

Gabriek. Where's Gabriek?

Somebody starts kicking me.

My eyes are shut but I know it's Cyryl because his screaming gets shriller each time his foot thuds into my ribs and tummy.

I hear my glasses being crushed against the cobblestones.

Men are still yelling and big fingers are trying to push their way into my mouth.

I realise the ring is still in there.

They're not having it. I keep my mouth closed. Hands go round my throat.

'Get away from him,' yells a voice.

Even with all the pain in my head I know it's Gabriek.

I open my eyes. Gabriek is close enough for me to see him clearly. He pulls himself away from the hands holding him and grabs the man choking me and flings him aside.

But another man raises a stick or a crowbar or something.

'Gabriek,' I croak.

Too late. There's a loud thud and Gabriek falls across me, heavy and limp.

He doesn't move.

Then the choking man is back. It's Mr Szynsky. He's in a frenzy to get his son's ring. I can tell he'll remove part of my face if he has to.

He can have the revolting ring. I just want him to leave me alone so I can look after Gabriek.

Before I can get the ring out of my mouth, somebody else starts shouting.

'Back away.'

Which the mob ignores. Until they hear a gunshot. Then everyone freezes.

Another gunshot.

Anya?

No, the voice is a man's.

I peer over Gabriek's slumped shoulder. I can just make out a military officer at the edge of the crowd. He's holding a pistol in the air. I can't tell what his uniform is. I hope it's not Russian or the Polish Secret Police or one of the other bad ones.

'Back off,' the officer yells again at the crowd.

They do, slowly.

The officer comes over, grabs Gabriek and pulls him to his feet. I'm relieved to see that after a bit of wobbling, Gabriek stays upright.

I get up too, wobbly as well.

'Let's get you out of here,' mutters the officer.

He speaks very bad Polish, but I understand him. As my dizziness goes, I also recognise him. He's the man from the truck that stopped earlier out on the road.

Mr Szynsky steps in front of the officer.

'I'm the mayor,' says Mr Szynsky in the voice people use when they want to sound important. He points at me. 'This vermin assaulted my son and robbed him.'

I can hear Cyryl whimpering nearby.

'You're the mayor?' says the officer.

Mr Szynsky nods, giving the officer a haughty look and me a look of hatred. Which changes to a look of surprise when the officer puts the barrel of his pistol against Mr Szynsky's forehead.

'Pleased to meet you, your worship,' says the officer in English. 'I was hoping I'd find the joker in authority who allowed this mob to get out of control. You're under arrest.'

He says the last bit in Polish.

Mr Szynsky stares at the officer, stunned and furious. He starts to say something about his brother-in-law being a government minister. But his voice is drowned out by the roar of an engine.

A horn starts blaring.

The officer's truck is coming slowly towards us through the crowd.

People scramble out of the way.

When the truck gets close, I see that driving it is the woman who was travelling with the officer.

'Get in,' says the officer to me and Gabriek, his gun still pointing at Mr Szynsky's head.

Gabriek opens the back flap of the truck.

All around us people are glaring and muttering. But they keep their distance.

Except for one man, small and plump and red-faced, who steps out of the crowd. Even without my glasses I can see he's got a rifle.

I spit the ring into my hand.

'Gabriek,' I yell. 'Look out.'

The man fires, turns, and disappears into the crowd.

The officer is on the ground.

'Help me, Felix,' yells Gabriek.

He grabs the officer's gun and points it at the

mob, and tries to pick the officer up one-handed.

I grab the officer's other arm and we half lift and half drag him into the back of the truck.

My head is spinning.

For a crazy second I thought it was Zliv with the gun. Except the gunman didn't look anything like a skinny version of Gogol. A small fat ex-Nazi more like.

Plus Zliv never misses his target. If that was Zliv, I'd be the one lying here in the back of the truck with a bullet in me.

'Drive,' yells Gabriek to the woman.

She doesn't move. She's sitting in the driver's seat, staring at the half-unconscious officer, at the blood all over his legs.

The crowd are shouting at us again and moving closer.

'Drive,' I yell at the woman in English, in case that's all she understands.

'Go,' yells Gabriek, also in English, and his voice suddenly sounds strange and weak.

I see why.

The back of his shirt is sodden with blood.

Which isn't the officer's blood. It's coming from Gabriek's head.

The woman revs the engine.

The truck lurches forward.

There's too much blood in here. I have to stop the bleeding.

If only my head wasn't throbbing so much.

I try not to think about it. I wasn't hit as hard as Gabriek. I'll be fine. I have to be. We need to get away from here.

Far away.

Maybe if I ask her nicely, the woman will slow down. So this truck won't bounce around so much. So I can stop all this bleeding.

I crawl closer to the driver's seat.

'Not so fast,' I yell.

I forget to say it in English, but it doesn't matter. The woman answers in Polish.

'We have to go as quickly as we can,' she shouts over her shoulder. 'The hospital's thirty miles away.'

That's too far. A human body only has about five litres of blood in it, which is ten litres total for Gabriek and the officer, and there's already about three on the floor of the truck.

'They both need medical attention now,' I yell. 'Urgently.'

The woman doesn't slow down.

I yell at her that there's no point going to a hospital if Gabriek and the officer die before we get there from all the bouncing.

'Apply pressure to the wounds,' she shouts. 'Lots of pressure.'

She's stubborn and pig-headed.

War can do that to people.

The woman speeds up even more. The sudden jolt of acceleration sends me sliding backwards.

Gabriek grabs me so I don't roll out the back of the truck. His chest is bare because he's taken his shirt off and wrapped it round his head.

'Let me see,' I say.

I take a look underneath.

The bruise on Gabriek's head is huge, but the cut isn't very deep. My hands are shaking from stress and bad truck suspension, but I manage to tie Gabriek's shirt tighter round his head, which will slow the bleeding even more.

'I'll be fine,' says Gabriek. 'It's not me we have to worry about.'

He points to the officer, who's lying on the truck floor in a big puddle of blood, groaning.

I slide over. I find the bullet hole in the officer's trouser leg and pull the cloth away as gently as I can and peer inside.

Even with the truck bouncing around and the canvas sides not letting much light in and me having to peer closely because I haven't got my glasses, I can see the officer's leg is bad.

The bullet has gone through his thigh.

From the amount of blood running out of the entry wound and also out of the exit hole on the other side, I'm guessing the bullet hit an artery or a major vein.

Gabriek helps me with pressure. I clamp my hands on one side of the officer's leg, Gabriek on the other side, squeezing as hard as we can.

It's not enough. Blood dribbles through our fingers.

'Clean and heat,' I say to Gabriek.

He knows what that means.

I've told him about the work I did with the partisans, helping Doctor Zajak.

But that was in the forest, not in the back of a speeding truck with no medical equipment.

I look around for some.

At first all I can see is a tyre lever strapped to the floor next to a spare tyre. Doctor Zajak did some big operations with not much equipment, but even he couldn't have stopped somebody from bleeding to death with a tyre lever.

Suddenly I feel weak and dizzy.

Which is only natural when you've been hit on the head and all your hopes and dreams for a safe happy life and possibly a regional university have been swept away by a vicious mob.

Plus I've just had Cyryl Szynsky's blood in my mouth, and that's enough to make anyone feel ill.

I tell myself to snap out of it. I peer around the back of the truck again. And see something behind the driver's seat.

The woman's handbag.

Perfect.

I get Gabriek to put his hands on both sides of the officer's leg.

'Keep as much pressure there as you can,' I say.

I crawl to the front of the truck and grab the bag. I don't ask the woman. She might not have heard about the high standard of medical care we gave the resistance fighters in the forest. She might think I'm just a kid who wants to muck around with her things.

I drag the bag over to the officer and look inside.

Excellent. Several of the things I was hoping for.

A pair of nail scissors and a hanky and a scarf and a nail file. And a packet of cigarettes, which means there'll be a lighter somewhere.

Yes, here it is.

'He's losing too much blood,' says Gabriek, squeezing the officer's leg so hard I'm worried about him popping veins. In the officer's leg and in his own head.

Quickly I pull the scarf out of the bag, roll it up and wedge it into the officer's mouth. Then I use the nail scissors to cut away the blood-sodden trousers from around the wound.

The hole in the officer's leg is quite big, but not big enough. I need to make it bigger so I can get my fingers inside and find the damaged vein.

I grip the scissors more tightly.

Oh no. I've got heat, but what about clean?

I rummage in the bag again.

At first all I find is a battered photograph frame with photos of little children tucked into it. Six or eight small faces.

That's strange, I think as I keep rummaging. The woman doesn't look old enough to have that many children.

Then I find what I'm looking for.

Perfume. Anya told me once that perfume is basically just alcohol and smelly stuff. Alcohol is good for a clean.

I pour some into the leg hole.

The officer's body jerks and he screams through the scarf. I'm glad Gabriek is holding him tight. From the look in the officer's eyes, he'd kill me if he could. Patients get like that sometimes.

I pour perfume onto the scissors, then start cutting the hole bigger.

The officer screams into the scarf again.

'What's going on?' yells the woman from the driver's seat.

'Lots of pressure,' I shout, so she'll think we're still following her advice. 'Keeping the pressure up.'

The pressure is up alright. Gabriek's fingers are white and my head is throbbing.

Now that the hole in the officer's leg is bigger, I can see the broken vein. I put perfume on my fingers, stick them into the hole and pinch the vein.

The officer's eyes go very big, then they close and suddenly he's floppy and limp.

'What's happened?' says Gabriek.

I check the officer's pulse with my other hand.

'He's OK,' I say. 'This is good. These sorts of operations are easier for patients when they faint.'

Gabriek looks doubtful.

'Heat,' I say to him.

Gabriek wraps the hanky from the bag around one end of the nail file. He starts heating the other end in the lighter flame.

After a few seconds I take the nail file from him and carefully lower it into the leg hole and touch the glowing tip against the broken end of the officer's vein. There's a loud hiss and smoke and the smell of cooking meat.

Yes.

The blood at the end of the vein is bubbling and going solid.

Doctor Zajak would be proud of me.

No he wouldn't. He'd see what I've forgotten to do and right now he'd be yelling at me.

No tourniquet. Nothing strapped around the officer's upper thigh to slow the blood flow to the wound so the end of the seared vein has a chance to harden and not leak.

'Pressure,' I yell at Gabriek and point to the place. Gabriek sees the problem. He puts his big hands around the officer's thigh.

I stand up and take my belt off and bend over and strap it tightly near Gabriek's hands.

Suddenly weakness and dizziness sweep over me even more than before.

Stop it, I say to myself. Stop feeling sorry for yourself. The farm was just a silly dream. This is what's really happening.

The truck hits a hole in the road.

I'm flung backwards.

My head smashes into something and the last thing I see is a flash so bright it's as if every farmhouse and every regional university in Poland is going up in flames.

Maybe this voice I'm hearing is real. And maybe the pain I'm feeling in my head and the rest of my body is real too.

Which means I'm not unconscious any more.

There were lots of other voices earlier, and lots of people prodding me, but it felt like I was dreaming most of that.

This voice sounds real.

'Felix,' it says, fuzzy and blurred, as if someone is putting their lips too close to my ear.

I keep my eyes shut so I can think.

I feel like I'm in a soft bed, which should be safe. But when you go unconscious in wartime, or even soon after, you can't be sure how much danger will be around when you wake up.

Before I open my eyes I get ready.

To fight. To run.

Because memories are coming back.

The truck. The blood.

The mob in the town square.

I don't know where I am. I don't know where Gabriek is. One thing I do know. We have to get as far away as we can from here.

I clench my fists.

When I was little I used to pray to the author of my favourite books. As I got older it felt silly, so I stopped. It doesn't feel silly now. Not when I think about the people in the town square.

'Felix,' says the voice again, still fuzzy.

Dear Richmal Crompton, I say silently. Please don't let this person with her lips close to my ear be a friend of the local people who attacked us and hurt Gabriek. Please let her be the truck woman who helped us get away. The one with the handbag and lots of children.

I open my eyes.

It's not the truck woman.

'Felix, at last,' says Anya, her lips still close to my ear. 'Thank God. Are you alright?'

I stare at Anya.

She shouldn't be here. She should be hiding in the woods.

'How many fingers am I holding up?' says Anya, stepping back from my pillow.

I don't care how many.

'Why aren't you in the woods?' I say.

'They came and found me,' says Anya.

I blink, trying to see who she means. We're in a big room, very glary. It's like a Nazi room where they keep the lights very bright until you confess.

I can just make out lots of blurred outlines of people who are whispering and hurrying around.

Why can't I see them better?

Of course, my glasses. They got crushed in the town square.

'Where's Gabriek?' I say to Anya.

I try to sit up.

Pain flashes through my head and insides.

'Take it easy,' says another voice.

Someone who looks like a nurse gently pushes more pillows behind me to prop me up.

'Don't worry, Felix,' says Anya. 'We're safe here.'

'Aha,' says a loud voice. 'Our hero is awake.'

A figure appears by my bed. An officer. Not the wounded one from the truck, a taller one with a moustache. His uniform looks English and he's speaking Polish with an accent.

'We're very grateful to you, young man,' he's saying. 'I'm Group Captain Thomas, commander of this air base. It seems you saved the life of one of my pilots. Please accept the gratitude of our entire military reconstruction team.'

'You're welcome,' I say. 'Is he alright?'

'Mending well,' says the commander, holding out his hand.

I think he wants me to shake it.

I do, which makes my ribs hurt.

'I'm told by my supervising medical officer,' says the commander, nodding towards a man next to him in a white medical coat, 'that you and your friend Mr Borowski have been examined and neither of you is in any immediate danger from your injuries. I'm very pleased to hear that.'

I'm very pleased to hear it too.

The supervising medical officer shines a light into my eyes.

'Still just a bit of concussion,' he says in English to the commander. 'Bed rest will fix it.'

I hope Gabriek is getting bed rest too. I squint around, trying to see him. There are other beds, but they're all too blurry.

'We're also told,' says the commander to me, 'by your young friend, that you need some glasses.'

I can't see Anya now. She must have moved away from the bed. She hasn't had very good experiences with military people, so she tries to stay away from them as much as possible.

'Yes, sir,' I say. 'I do.'

'Please accept some with our compliments,' says the commander.

A younger officer in an American uniform comes over with a cardboard box.

Inside are about twenty pairs of glasses.

'Take your time,' says the younger officer. 'The staff and aircrew here were very touched when they heard how you saved Flight Lieutenant Wagstaff. So they took up a collection. All their spare specs. Choose whichever pair suits you. Two pairs if you like.'

He speaks Polish almost perfectly. I wish we'd had his language teacher when me and Anya were learning English.

I try the glasses on.

Most of them are too big or too blurry. But finally I find a pair that fit and that work as well as my old pair. Better, because the old ones had a crack in them from shrapnel.

'Thank you,' I say to the doctors and nurses and orderlies, who I can see clearly now.

They all clap.

I know it's rude not to have more of a proper conversation with people who've just given you a very useful gift, but now that I can see again, I just want to find Gabriek.

I peer around the ward.

And see him, standing a few beds away, giving me a thumbs up.

Gabriek doesn't look weak or sick. Not even concussed. The shirt we put round his head must have done the trick. Somebody's replaced it with a bandage, which isn't showing any blood leaks at all. Which is a big relief. When the Nazis burned Gabriek's farmhouse down, part of the roof fell on his head so I'm always nervous about him getting more head injuries.

I give Gabriek a wave, then look for Anya.

She's standing on the other side of the ward. She gives me a thumbs up too.

'Felix,' says the officer with the cardboard box.

'When Flight Lieutenant Wagstaff comes out of intensive care tomorrow, he'll want to thank you personally. Until then, if there's anything you need from our medical staff, just let them know.'

I think for a few moments.

'Actually,' I say, 'there is something.'

The officer waits for me to continue. But it's medical and private, so I'd rather not say it to him.

I give the supervising medical officer a look and he comes over.

'What is it, Felix?' he says in very bad Polish.

I glance across at Anya.

I know this is involving her with the military, but it's important, so I don't think she'll mind.

'My friend Anya has been pregnant for seven and a half months,' I say to him, 'and she's never had a medical examination. Can she have one here?'

I say it in English, because I want to be sure he understands.

The supervising medical officer looks over at Anya, frowning.

I hope I didn't use the wrong words. When we learned English, all we had apart from the baby book was a Polish-English dictionary, a Hungarian neighbour with a pen-friend in Yorkshire, and two Richmal Crompton books in English which I read out over and over to Anya.

It was OK, but it wasn't perfect.

The supervising medical officer turns to the commander.

'Sir,' he says, 'it is irregular, an examination of a pregnant civilian, but I'm happy to arrange it with your permission.'

He's speaking English too, but I can understand most of the words.

Before the commander can reply, I jump in again. Gabriek always says it's best if people only have to say yes once.

'And afterwards,' I say to the supervising medical officer, 'can Anya have the baby here?'

The supervising medical officer looks startled.

The commander frowns.

'This is a military air base,' he says. 'It is not a facility for the birth of babies. Right, Langtry?'

'I suppose not if you say so, sir,' mutters the supervising medical officer.

I think the supervising medical officer is on our side. Which is good. He'd be perfect to deliver Anya's baby.

'We don't mind,' I say to the commander in Polish. 'A ditch at the side of the road isn't a facility for the birth of babies either.'

The commander glares at me.

I should repeat it in English for the supervising medical officer. While I'm trying to think of the English word for ditch, somebody else speaks up in Polish.

'Excuse me, Group Captain, I think I can help.'

The commander turns. Stepping towards him is the woman who drove the truck.

'I'm a nurse,' she says. 'Well, I used to be. But I've helped with a lot of births, so if I can be of assistance with this young woman, I'd be glad to.'

The commander looks at her crossly.

'Do you work here?' he says.

The woman shakes her head.

'Well,' says the commander, 'I don't know why you're here, but I'll thank you not to interfere.'

The woman shrinks a bit and looks at the floor.

I struggle to sit up. It must be a stressful job, being part of a military reconstruction team, but having a bit of stress is no excuse for being rude and unkind.

Zelda taught me that.

'This brave lady,' I say to the commander, 'is here because she rescued us. Me and Gabriek and your pilot. So please be nice to her.'

The commander is frowning again. I think he's feeling ashamed of himself. But I can't be certain because sitting up and speaking loudly has made me feel very dizzy.

I flop back onto the pillows.

The supervising medical officer hurries over and takes my pulse.

'You mustn't over-excite yourself, Felix,' he says. 'You're suffering from concussion. You need to be as calm and rested as possible.'

He's speaking English, but I understand perfectly. He's a nice doctor who is concerned about me and wants me to get better.

Which is very kind of him.

He signals to a nurse.

I see Gabriek coming towards my bed. Before he arrives, a needle is pricked into my arm.

My eyelids start to feel heavy.

Gabriek is looking concerned.

So is Anya.

As my eyes close I don't feel concerned at all.

We're in a friendly air base with good military security, excellent medical facilities, superb heating and almost certainly plenty of food. The people here don't really know us yet, but when I show them Gabriek's fixing skills and Anya's organising skills and more of my medical skills, I'm pretty sure they'll let us live here, safe from violent mobs, for as long as we like.

Maybe those fried potatoes I can smell are for me. I think they are.

I love fried potatoes for breakfast.

Thanks, Mum. Thanks, Dad.

I rub my eyes like I often do before I completely wake up. And I start feeling the sadness I always feel when sleep goes and painful memories come back.

If Zelda was here now, I know what she'd say.

'Your mummy and daddy love you very much,' she'd say. 'But people can't fry potatoes after they're dead. Don't you know anything?'

I open my eyes.

My bed and the rest of the ward are bright with early morning sunlight.

Under my nose is a big white china plate.

I reach for my new glasses and put them on and stare at what's on the plate.

Potato slices, crispy and fragrant.

And toast glistening with what looks like actual creamy butter. And three fried eggs. That's more eggs than I've had on the same plate ever in my life.

'Hello, Felix,' says a voice.

I look up.

Crouching next to my bed, holding the plate under my chin, is a man in a dark suit.

I don't know him, but I'm thinking I'd like to. As well as offering me a delicious breakfast, he's also giving me a friendly smile.

'Hello,' I say.

An exciting thought hits me.

Perhaps the air base people have already decided that me and Gabriek and Anya look like we'd be useful around the place, and a delicious breakfast is their way of saying they'd like us to stay.

'How are you feeling?' says the man.

His Polish is almost as bad as the supervising medical officer's. And his accent is the same as the officer who was shot.

'Good, thank you,' I say.

My head is aching and my bruised ribs are hurting, but I'm sure they'll feel better once I've had the creamy butter and the three eggs.

'Are you American?' I say.

I'm speaking English to be friendly.

The man smiles and shakes his head.

'Australian,' he says. 'My name's Ken.'

He shakes my hand, puts the plate onto a tray and signals to a nurse.

She comes over and helps me sit up. Which hurts, but the pain doesn't seem so bad once she puts the tray on my lap.

'Thank you,' I say.

There's a bowl on the tray as well. With lumps of something yellowy-orange in it. I sniff the lumps. They smell a bit like turnip, only sweeter.

'Taste it,' says Ken.

I do. The lumps are very sweet and much more delicious than turnip.

'Mango,' says Ken, sitting down next to my bed. 'Lots of it in Australia. Lots of eggs and potatoes too.'

I gobble more of the mango. All I know about Australia is that it's a long way away. Now I also know it has delicious fruit.

'Would you like to go to Australia?' says Ken.

I look at him, not sure how to answer.

Does he mean if the world was a different place and I was very rich and important and older?

'You can go to Australia later this week if you like,' says Ken.

I stare at him, stunned.

He says it again, in Polish.

A lump of mango plops out of my mouth onto the tray.

'Before you answer,' says Ken, 'let me tell you a bit about Australia. OK if I go back to speaking English? My Polish isn't so hot, plus I want to give you some practice with our lingo.'

I nod, dazed.

I didn't understand all of that last bit, but I understood enough. When Ken stuns you, he does it slowly, which helps.

'We're very lucky in Australia,' says Ken. 'Our country came out of the war mostly undamaged. Few Jap bombs, couple of subs lobbing shells, that was about it. Nowhere near as wrecked as Europe.'

He pauses to see if I understand.

Australian is quite different to English, but I'm getting most of it.

I nod.

'However,' says Ken, 'we did cop another type of damage. A lot of Aussies came over here to Europe to fight the Nazis. Quite a few got killed. As you can imagine, their families are pretty sad about never seeing them again.'

I nod again. I don't have to imagine. I know what that feels like.

What I don't know is why Ken is telling me all this. And why he's offering me a trip to Australia.

I ask him.

Ken smiles, as if he's glad I did.

'I work for the Australian government,' he says, still speaking slowly. 'My job is to help people back home feel better about the war. Which is why in a couple of days we're flying one of our warplanes back there. So we can take it around the country and give the folks a first-hand gander at what their heroes have been up to. Which is where you come in, Felix. Eat your eggs before they get cold.'

I stare at the eggs. I'd forgotten about them.

I eat. It gives me a chance to work out what some of the words mean. But the more I translate them, the more confused I feel.

'Doug Wagstaff told me about you,' says Ken. 'You know, the pilot you saved.'

'Did he say that I'd be good at cheering up sad Australians?' I ask.

Ken smiles.

'I've been looking for someone like you,' he says. 'A youngster who made it through. Someone who owes his life to the Allied victory. To the Brits and the Yanks and the Aussies. Someone who'd be dead if the Nazis had won. And who also speaks English. We reckon that the people of Australia will enjoy meeting you a lot, Felix. And hearing you talk about yourself. You'll help Aussies understand that they lost their loved ones for a very good reason.'

Ken stops and looks at me closely.

'Do you understand?' he says.

'Yes,' I say after a while. 'Mostly. You want me to be very grateful. And bring tears to the eyes of Australian people. Sad tears and happy tears.'

Ken grins.

'Spot on,' he says. 'And you won't regret it, Felix. Australia is a wonderful place. Great food. Great sport. Great beaches. Great girls. Bet you understand that last bit, right?'

I try to think of the words in English to explain a few things to Ken that he got wrong.

Not language things.

Fact things.

Such as how I mostly owe my life to Mum and Dad and Zelda and Genia and all the other people who've given me good protection.

And how with Gabriek and Anya watching my back, there's a chance I wouldn't be dead even if the Nazis had won.

But I change my mind. I don't say any of that.

I put some egg into my mouth instead.

Because I'm imagining something incredible and very exciting. Me and Gabriek and Anya and the baby living in Australia. A quiet place that hasn't been smashed and ruined by war. Where the people are still friendly and kind. Somewhere so far away, Zliv probably hasn't even heard of it.

Thinking of Zliv makes me glance around.

The ward is almost empty. Just a couple of nurses and a couple of patients.

Gabriek and Anya aren't here.

I'm hoping Anya is off somewhere having her medical examination, but where's Gabriek?

'Where are they?' I say to Ken. 'My friends?'

'It's OK,' says Ken. 'They're staying nearby. With Celeste Prejenka.'

I stare at him.

I haven't got a clue who Celeste Prejenka is.

'The girlfriend of the wounded pilot,' says Ken. 'She drove you here in the truck, right? Last night she offered your friends a place to stay.'

'They should be staying here,' I say. 'Where it's safe.'

'Civilians can't stay on a military base,' says Ken. 'Not unless they have a personal invitation from the commanding officer. And the CO here doesn't like civilians.'

I open my mouth to protest.

'Your friends are safe at Celeste's,' says Ken. 'Her neighbours are all staff from the base. Those thugs from town wouldn't get within half a mile of her place. And her cottage is much more comfortable than here.'

I think about this.

Celeste Prejenka said she used to be a nurse. Maybe she can give Anya a medical examination. And if Celeste's neighbours are as protective as Ken says, maybe Zliv wouldn't be able to get within half a mile of the place either.

Maybe.

'So,' says Ken. 'What do you say? Fancy a new life in Australia?'

'Before I decide,' I tell him, 'there are two things I want.'

'Anything,' says Ken. 'Fire away.'

'First,' I say, 'I want Flight Lieutenant Wagstaff to have a breakfast like this one.'

Ken smiles.

'Got you,' he says. 'It's hungry work, right, saving people from violent mobs. What's the other thing?'

'I need to talk with Gabriek and Anya,' I say. 'Now. This morning.'

Ken pats me on the arm.

'Of course,' he says. 'Big thing, saying goodbye to friends.'

I look at him, puzzled.

'If I go to Australia,' I say, 'Gabriek and Anya will come with me.'

Ken sighs.

'That's not possible, Felix,' he says. 'Sorry, but it's out of the question. We must leave this week. That young lady can't fly till after she's had her baby. And your friend Gabriek can't fly at all, not with his medical condition.'

I stare at Ken, hoping I've got the words wrong.

But I haven't.

I know the English words for 'medical condition'. I've read them lots of times in the baby book.

'Medical condition?' I say to Ken. 'What medical condition?'

He sighs again.

I can see he wishes he hadn't mentioned it.

Too late.

'What medical condition?' I yell.

There's been a mix-up.

That's what I keep saying to myself while I wait for Ken to get back with the supervising medical officer.

Ken isn't medically trained.

He probably doesn't understand the difference between 'medical condition' and 'complete medical cure'. Specially if a nurse is trying to explain it to him in Polish.

I'm still clinging to that thought when Ken and the supervising medical officer arrive at my bed.

Ken stands back. The supervising medical officer gives me a nervous smile.

'Feeling better?' he says.

'There's been a very big mistake,' I say to him in English. 'Ken thinks that Gabriek has got a medical condition.'

The supervising medical officer sighs and looks unhappy. Which doesn't make me feel the slightest bit better.

'What's going on?' I say, my voice loud with fear and squeaky with panic.

The supervising medical officer sits down next to my bed.

'Felix,' he says, speaking English slowly. 'In the past, Gabriek had a head injury, didn't he?'

'Yes,' I say. 'The Nazis burned his farmhouse. Some of the roof fell on him. But that was over a year ago. He's been fine.'

'Until yesterday,' says the supervising medical officer. 'That blow on the head he received in the town square, plus his earlier injury, has left him with a serious condition.'

This place isn't so superbly heated after all.

I'm shivering.

'It's not all bad news, Felix,' says the supervising medical officer. 'There is no immediate danger for Gabriek. If he looks after himself, he won't die. Probably he'll live a long and happy life. But only if he stays away from big and sudden changes in air pressure. So no flying and no deep-sea diving.'

'Do you understand?' says Ken.

I nod numbly.

'No flying,' I say. 'No deep diving in the sea.'

Ken smiles. Probably because he thinks we don't do deep-sea diving in Poland.

We do. So he's wrong. They both are.

'There must be an operation,' I say desperately. 'Something that will cure Gabriek. Or make it less serious. So he can fly.'

The supervising medical officer hesitates.

He looks even more unhappy.

'There is an operation,' he says. 'But I'm not qualified to do it. It's a difficult and very specialised procedure. I doubt there are any surgeons left in Poland who could do it. And almost no hospitals with the necessary facilities intact.'

'Too fast,' mutters Ken. 'Say it slower.'

The supervising medical officer starts saying it all again.

I understood the first time.

I don't bother waiting for him to finish.

'I'll do the operation,' I say. 'I'll learn how to, and I'll get the facilities, and I'll do it.'

I glare at Ken.

Just let him dare smile at that.

He doesn't.

'Felix,' says the supervising medical officer, more slowly this time. 'I saw the work you did on Flight Lieutenant Wagstaff's leg. Rough, but very impressive. You're going to be a fine doctor. But not in Poland. Most of our universities are destroyed. Very few medical schools have survived. The sons of rich families are taking all the places. You need to find somewhere that has better opportunities. Which, Felix, is why you should go to Australia.'

I glare at him.

He and Ken must be friends.

They're in this together.

'Also,' says the supervising medical officer, 'there are your legs.'

I keep glaring at him.

'What about my legs?' I say.

'The muscular-skeletal condition you have can be treated,' says the supervising medical officer. 'Australia has surgeons who could possibly do that. Worth thinking about, eh?'

I don't reply. I don't trust him.

I struggle out of bed, ignoring the pain in my ribs, and start taking my hospital pyjamas off.

'What are you doing?' says the supervising medical officer.

'Where are my clothes?' I say. 'There's somewhere I need to be.'

The supervising medical officer calls for nurses

and a couple of them hurry over and put me back into bed.

Nurses are stronger than they look.

What the people here don't realise is that I'm more determined than I look.

'Take it easy, Felix,' says Ken. 'No rush. Plenty of time for goodbyes. We're not leaving for Australia for a couple of days.'

'And,' says the supervising medical officer, 'the flight can probably be delayed for a day or two more if you need extra time to recover.'

I give them both a long look.

They're probably both very well educated. Australia and England have probably got lots of very good universities without the slightest bit of bomb damage. Ken and the supervising medical officer probably both spent years studying there and learned lots.

But if they think I'm going to Australia without Gabriek and Anya, they don't know anything.

Maybe that's Celeste Prejenka's house there.

The person on the corner said it was down here somewhere and it's the only one with light flickering in the windows. All I can see in the rest of this lane are a few dark cottages and lots of dark trees.

As I get closer to the glowing house, the moon goes behind a cloud.

I walk carefully through the mud, trying not to make my ribs hurt more. After the effort I put into getting away from the hospital, I don't want to crack something and end up back in the ward.

I don't think discharging myself would work again. I think the guards will be checking the back of laundry trucks leaving the air base much more closely from now on.

The moon comes out again.

I make my way up a path towards a front door. Yes, this looks like the right house.

On the doorstep are Gabriek's and Anya's boots.

And another pair which must be Celeste Prejenka's.

But no children's boots.

I sigh.

You know how sometimes in wartime people have lots of children so if a few get killed they'll still have some left but war is so brutal that sometimes all the children get killed and parents are just left with photographs?

I think that might have happened to Celeste Prejenka.

I knock on the door.

Celeste Prejenka opens it.

'Hello,' I say sympathetically.

She frowns at me.

'Shouldn't you be in hospital?' she says. 'You're meant to be under observation for concussion.'

'I discharged myself,' I say. 'I'm hoping that with my medical experience and yours, I could be under observation here, if that's alright with you.'

Celeste smiles.

She doesn't argue. We both know there are much more serious things that can happen than a bit of concussion.

'Come in,' she says. 'A little medical observation is the least I can offer after scaring you on the road like that.'

At first I think she means her very fast driving. Then I realise she means the first time I met her, when she and Flight Lieutenant Wagstaff stopped their truck on the road and she was weird.

'I must apologise,' says Celeste. 'I was feeling upset that day. And then as we drove past, I thought I recognised you. Stupid. My memory plays tricks on me sometimes.'

'That's OK,' I say. 'Mine does too sometimes.'

Celeste leads me into a little sitting room.

Gabriek and Anya must have heard my voice because they're standing up. I can tell from the way the candles are flickering that they jumped up quickly. Which isn't good for people with their medical conditions.

'Sit down,' I say to them. 'Relax. I'm not rushing off anywhere.'

I want them to know that. Just in case they've heard about Ken's offer and think I've accepted and have come to say goodbye.

As if.

Now I'm the one who needs to sit down.

After what Gabriek has just been saying, my legs have almost stopped working.

I slump onto a chair.

Gabriek and Anya sit down too.

They look at me, concerned.

'We wish we could all go together,' says Gabriek. 'But it's important that you go now.'

'Gabriek's right,' says Anya.

'That's totally crazy,' I say. 'You've both gone mad. There's no way I'm going to Australia without you.'

This is what I'd feared.

Ken must have talked to Gabriek at the hospital. Filled his head with crazy ideas.

Gabriek's obviously got concussion worse than me. I should go and get Celeste from the kitchen so we can examine him together.

'Felix,' says Gabriek. 'Think about it sensibly. Anya can't fly in her condition. I can't either. But we can both come later. The Australian government is working on a plan to increase the population of their country. They're going to start taking people from Europe. By boat. Completely free of charge. In a year or so.'

'Good,' I say. 'That's when we'll all go.'

Gabriek sighs.

'Ken is offering you a precious opportunity now, Felix,' he says. 'You'll meet people who can help you with your education. Australia has some of the best universities in the world. Sydney University. Melbourne University.'

'Ken showed you brochures, did he?' I mutter. 'He really knows how to twist you round his finger, doesn't he?'

Gabriek looks hurt.

'Felix,' says Anya. 'Don't be a jerk.'

She's right. Normally I'd say sorry to Gabriek for being rude and unkind.

But I'm too upset. All the special people in my life except for Gabriek and Anya have gone.

Gabriek said we're in this together.

Two days ago he said it.

And now Gabriek and Anya want us not to be in this together for a whole year.

'I'm not going,' I say to Anya. 'I'm not leaving you to have the baby on your own.'

Anya looks at me.

'You're a dear sweet friend,' she says. 'But you're also an idiot. We need you to grab this chance and get yourself set up in Australia. So when you meet the three of us off the boat in a year's time, you'll have somewhere to take us. And you'll know what's what and where's where. And we won't all be sitting in the gutter scratching our heads.'

I start to tell her how totally crazy that is, but I stop. Because it's not.

Not totally.

'I'll be fine having the baby,' says Anya. 'Thanks to your book and all the talking we've done about cervixes and placentas and things. And Celeste has lots of experience.'

I stare at the floor.

I try to imagine what it would be like not to see Gabriek or Anya for a year.

I could do it, of course I could.

But I don't want to.

'We'll miss you, Felix,' says Anya.

She gives me one of her looks and even though I'm very cross, my insides go softer than butter on a breakfast plate.

'Sleep on it, Felix,' says Gabriek quietly. 'You don't have to decide tonight.'

'Good idea,' I say.

It is a good idea because tomorrow I won't be so tired and my head won't be hurting and I can deal with this nonsense once and for all.

Tomorrow I can remind Gabriek and Anya of the main reason I won't be going to Australia. The most important reason I won't be leaving them here on their own.

A reason I don't even want to think about just before going to bed.

So I'm not even going to say his name.

Maybe I'm hearing things. Maybe concussion can make your ears go strange.

I wonder if Gabriek and Anya can hear that scary sound.

'Gabriek,' I whisper.

Nothing.

Only the murmur of his steady breathing.

I sit up. Celeste's sitting room is dark. The fireplace is just embers. Thick curtains on the windows. No moonlight at all.

Gabriek and Anya are lying next to me on the floor, still asleep.

I hear the sound again.

Footsteps on the soft mud outside. Made by somebody who doesn't want to be heard.

Somebody who never gives up.

I hold my breath. I think about where I can find a weapon, fast.

Anya's gun is probably in her coat pocket.

That's if the guards at the air base didn't take it. Probably not. Anya is very good at using her pregnant tummy to distract people.

There's the sound again.

I reach for Anya's coat.

Wait a minute. There's a flicker of light under Celeste's bedroom door. The sound is coming from inside her room.

It's only Celeste.

I breathe out with relief.

Zliv hasn't found us. Not yet.

But how long till he does? A neighbour in the city told me that Zliv once waited four months to kill a Serbian warlord who stole from him. He tracked the warlord across two countries, then waited until the river Danube thawed so he could swim underwater to the warlord's hideout with a knife in his mouth.

Next morning the warlord was found dead in his bed. With his skin missing.

I shiver.

I shouldn't be thinking about this.

Yes I should. Because one night, sooner or later, I'll hear a sound and it won't be a kind ex-nurse in the next room.

I wriggle back under my blanket and shut my eyes and try to breathe slowly. It's something the partisans taught me.

I almost manage to. Until a thought hits me.

A thought so crazy it makes me sit up again.

It's an idea about Zliv. What I could do about him if I go to Australia.

No, it's too risky. Much too dangerous.

But it might work.

Maybe.

I push the thought out of my mind because I'm hearing the sound again. Still coming from Celeste's room. But now it's not like footsteps at all.

More like slow painful sobbing.

I slip out from under the blanket, careful not to wake Gabriek and Anya. I put my glasses on and move slowly over to the bedroom door and listen.

Celeste is crying.

It's none of my business. After a war, the world is probably full of sad and unhappy people who cry by themselves at night.

But sometimes having the right person with you can help.

I don't know what it feels like to have all your children killed. I don't know how a parent could live with that. But I do know how it feels to miss people very much.

I tap on the door.

It's not locked. It swings open.

I stand in the doorway.

Celeste is sitting on the floor in front of a small table with candles burning on it.

Her head is in her hands.

This is private. I should really close the door and leave.

But it's too late. I've already started thinking about Mum and Dad and Zelda. If they were here I know for certain they wouldn't leave this poor person to sob on her own.

I go over to Celeste and kneel down and put my hand on her shoulder.

For a moment she doesn't do anything.

Then she looks at me. Her face is puzzled. She doesn't seem to recognise me at first. She brushes wet hair out of her eyes.

'Felix,' she says. 'What's wrong?'

I can see what's wrong. On the table are eight small candles burning in eight small saucers. In front of each candle is a photograph of a child.

Eight of them.

Eight small children.

Celeste sees me looking at the photos. She tries to say something. But a sob catches in her throat and her face is full of anguish.

My hand is still on her shoulder.

I leave it there.

'We have to look after each other,' I say. 'The Nazis killed our families, so we have to.'

Celeste doesn't reply. Just stares at the photos.

When she does speak her voice is so small and shaky, I'm not sure if I'm hearing her properly.

'The Nazis didn't kill my children,' she says.

I look at her, puzzled.

She turns to me.

'I killed them,' she says.

Tears are rolling down her face. My heart is thudding loudly.

'I'm sorry,' she says. 'I shouldn't have told you that. It's not fair. You're just a boy. You shouldn't have to hear that.'

I'm in shock. I don't know what to say.

One thing I do know.

In wartime things are never simple. Good things get mixed up with bad things. Sometimes it's hard to tell which is which.

'I'm still listening,' I say to Celeste, my voice as shaky as hers.

Celeste hesitates.

She looks at the photographs again.

'I was a nurse in a Jewish children's hospital,' she says. 'We were planning to evacuate the children before the Nazis arrived. But the Nazis advanced too quickly. One day they were suddenly in the city, in our district, and minutes later they were outside the hospital.'

Celeste pauses.

On her face is the effort of the words.

'The children were all too sick to walk,' she says. 'It was too late to carry them. The other nurses and me, we'd agreed what we'd do if this happened. We'd agreed we wouldn't let the Nazis get their hands on our children. We wouldn't let our children be killed in a painful way.'

Celeste stops and just breathes for a while.

I can see how hard it is for her to do even that.

'We heard the Nazis trying to smash the door in,' she says. 'We had a tiny amount of morphine left. We gave it to the children. But it wasn't enough. All it did was put them to sleep. So we got pillows and held the children in our arms and made sure the Nazis would never be able to hurt them.'

She stops again.

So much pain on her gentle face.

'Then,' says Celeste, 'we cut our wrists. My cuts weren't deep enough. The other nurses died, but I woke up.'

A sob escapes from her throat

I don't say anything.

Just put my arms round her.

'The Nazis beat me,' she says. 'For spoiling their plans. Called me murdering scum. I agreed with them. They put me in a slave labour camp. I thought I'd die there. I should have done, but I didn't.'

She presses her face into my shoulder and more sobs shake her.

I wait till she finishes.

'You did your best,' I say softly. 'I knew someone else who did something like that. He was doing his best too. He was a good person like you.'

Celeste pulls away. Looks me in the face.

'I'm not a good person, Felix,' she says.

Her eyes are so sad. Again I don't know what to say. I wish I had the words. I wish I could say something to help her feel better.

'Do you have any family?' I say.

It's a risky thing to ask in wartime, but I want her to have somebody. Somebody who understands. Somebody who forgives her. Somebody who can help her see her own good heart.

A fourteen-year-old person you've only just met isn't enough.

'Before the war,' says Celeste, 'my father died and my mother went to live in Australia. Our plan was for me to join her in Melbourne. But the war started and I was trapped here in Poland. We managed to keep in touch for a while. Then we lost contact for six years. When the war ended I tried to get in touch again. But I didn't ever hear back. She must have moved. I haven't been able to find her. She probably thinks I'm dead.'

Celeste stares at the floor.

I have a thought. About how wars can really mess up postal deliveries, but not always.

'In your letters,' I say, 'did you tell your mother what happened? With the children in the hospital? And then afterwards?'

Maybe a letter got through. Maybe her mother is trying to find her. To hold her. To forgive her.

Celeste shakes her head.

'I can't put that in a letter,' she says. 'I need to tell her that myself.'

I look at the pain and sadness on Celeste's face. A mother would understand, I know she would. A mother would put her arms round her daughter and they'd be much better arms than mine.

I have another thought.

'Your friend Flight Lieutenant Wagstaff,' I say. 'He's Australian. He could take you.'

Celeste sighs.

'That was my plan,' she says. 'My selfish plan. When I heard there was an Australian pilot in the district, and I found out he was going to fly a special plane back to Australia, I made sure I met him and made friends with him.'

She looks away.

I think she must be embarrassed about having a romance for travel purposes.

'It's OK,' I say. 'Most people would do that to find their mum.'

Celeste sighs again.

'Dougie was going to smuggle me onto the flight to Australia,' she says. 'But he can't do that now. His leg won't heal for ages. They're bringing in another pilot.'

My mind is racing.

'You can still go,' I say. 'Ken will take you. You can be his special survivor. You can be the one to meet the people of Australia. And after that you can find your mother.'

Celeste shakes her head miserably.

'I asked Ken yesterday,' she says. 'I begged him. But I'm too old. He wants a young survivor.'

I stare at her.

That's ridiculous. Celeste can't be any more than thirty. What's wrong with a middle-aged survivor?

'It's not just my age,' says Celeste. 'I'd have to talk about myself to the newspapers over there. I don't think the Australian people would feel very good discovering that their sons and husbands had died to save a woman who killed eight children.'

It's alright, I want to say to her.

They'd understand.

But then I remember that people who haven't actually been in a war often don't understand.

Unless they're your mother.

I think about Mum.

I imagine telling her some of the things that I've done. Things I'm ashamed of. Times I've been selfish. Times I've been scared. Times I haven't been able to save people.

I imagine Mum's arms around me.

Forgiving me.

Celeste's eyes are full of tears again. So are mine.

I hear the sound of floorboards creaking.

It's not me or Celeste.

The bedroom door is open. Gabriek and Anya are standing in the doorway, gazing at Celeste, almost in tears themselves.

They look at me. They don't say anything.

They don't need to.

I nod slowly to let them know that I'm going to Australia.

Maybe it's not too late to pull out. To cancel the trip. To tell Ken I'm not going to Australia.

Not in this monster.

I stare up at the huge dark plane standing at the end of the runway. Its giant wings and engines blocking out the sky.

A Lancaster bomber, Ken says it's called.

'Once you've seen one, you'll never forget it,' he said this morning in the air-base briefing room.

I didn't realise then, but I'd already seen one. More than one. And he's right, I won't ever forget. Not ever. Hundreds of them filling the night sky. Their deafening noise making babies scream and cows vomit. Their bombs turning the homes of innocent families into brick-dust and mincemeat.

OK, they were aiming at Nazis. Most of the time. But still.

Do I really have to go up in this monster?

I pull myself together. I've promised Celeste.

Plus it's the only way I can keep Gabriek and Anya safe. To deal with Zliv once and for all.

A hand whacks me on the shoulder.

'Photos,' says Ken, hurrying past in his flying suit with his briefcase under his arm. 'Let the folks in Australia know you're on your way.'

He waves me over to a photographer who has a camera set up on a tripod.

I waddle across, trying not to trip over. I haven't got used to these flying boots yet.

Ken smooths the creases out of my flying jacket and steps back. The photographer shows me where to stand, then peers through his camera.

'Try to look heroic,' says Ken. 'But also grateful. Like you're thinking of all the brave Aussies who sacrificed themselves for your freedom.'

I try.

The photographer takes a few photos, thanks me and starts to pack up.

'Last goodbyes, Felix,' says Ken. 'We leave in ten.'

He means minutes. Part of me wishes he meant hours. Or months.

'Ken,' I say, but he's already walking away, too busy to hear me.

He'd better not have been too busy to talk to the commander. To fix it so that if Anya and Celeste need medical help with the birth, the base hospital will provide it.

Ken frowned this morning when I told him that was the deal.

'Not gunna be easy,' he said. 'The base hospital's not kitted out for childbirth.'

I didn't understand all the Australian words, but I could tell from Ken's face what he meant.

'They don't need anything special,' I said. 'Just hot water and a sharp pair of scissors. Talk to the commander or I'm not going.'

'Okey doke,' said Ken, rolling his eyes. 'I'll fix it.'

I hope this air base is better at childbirth than they are at organising.

This runway is chaos. People in uniform running around with clipboards. Other people in overalls doing things to the plane. There's oil dripping from one of the engines and I think that's a puddle of aircraft fuel on the tarmac.

I watch the ground crew struggling to load big kitbags into the machine-gun turret at the back of the plane.

Crazy. They'd be better off taking the machine gun out first. We're not going to need it. Anya could organise things better than this standing on her head.

I look around to see if Anya has arrived. Gabriek and Celeste are walking towards me, alone.

'Where's Anya?' I say.

Celeste gives an apologetic shrug.

My insides droop.

'Doesn't she want to say goodbye?' I say.

Gabriek swaps a glance with Celeste. It's a very quick one, but I see it.

Is something wrong? Has Anya changed her mind about me going? Is she not here because she's upset and wants me to stay?

'Try not to feel bad, Felix,' says Gabriek, putting his arm round my shoulders. 'The four of us have spent the last two days saying goodbye. Maybe Anya's just said all hers.'

'For now,' says Celeste, stroking my hair.

I pull myself together.

Plenty of time for feeling sad later. There are other more important things to do now.

'Don't forget,' I say to Gabriek, 'that Ken will be sending you a special letter from the Australian government that guarantees places for you and Celeste and Anya and the baby on the first boat to Australia.'

Gabriek smiles.

'I won't forget,' he says. 'Because you've told me fifty times.'

'Hey, Felix,' yells Ken from near the plane. 'Time to get on board.'

I look at Gabriek. His weatherbeaten face is so full of love, I can hardly bear this.

'No deep-sea diving,' I say to him.

It's meant to be a joke, but my voice is so sad it sounds like I'm the one under water.

Gabriek doesn't say anything.

Just gives my shoulders a long squeeze, his eyes not leaving my face.

'Whoa,' yells a voice in English. 'Not so fast.'

I look around.

A nurse is pushing a man in a wheelchair across the tarmac towards us. The man is waving wildly.

As he gets closer, I see that one of his legs is heavily bandaged.

Then I recognise him.

'Hello, Flight Lieutenant Wagstaff,' I say.

'Dougie,' says the man, holding out his hand. 'Didn't want the plane taking off before I could say thanks.'

I shake his hand. I'm very pleased to see him. When I tried to visit him yesterday to thank him for saving us, he was having surgery again.

'Thank you, Dougie,' I say. 'I hope your leg gets better.'

'No worries,' says Dougie. 'I'll be surfing before Christmas.'

I'm not sure what that means, but I'm glad he seems so cheerful. When I'm doing photos in Australia, and they ask me to think of Aussies making sacrifices, I'll think of Dougie.

'If you ever find yourself in Coonabarabran,' says Dougie, 'go to the Civic Hotel and draw them a diagram of what you did to my leg and they'll buy you drinks for a week.'

He speaks so fast I miss some of it, but I can tell it's something kind.

'Thank you,' I say.

'No,' says Dougie. 'Thank you.'

There are four men with him in flying suits.

'So,' says one of them, grinning at me. 'This must be our cargo.'

'VIP cargo, mate,' says Dougie to the man. 'And don't you forget it.'

I don't know what VIP means but the others seem to. They all roll their eyes.

'This is Rusty, your pilot,' says Dougie to me. 'Simmo the flight engineer, Gav the navigator, and Wally the wireless operator when he's sober.'

I understand most of that, and I try to look like I understand it all.

'Hello,' I say to them.

They all mutter things that sound like 'gerday'.

'Make sure you look after this one,' says Dougie to Rusty. 'No bumps, right?'

'I've got a rule, Dougie,' says Rusty. 'No bumps, no bullets. Pity you didn't adopt that motto.'

I'm confused, but they all laugh, which is good. They seem friendly.

'Let's get you on the plane,' Rusty says to me.

I turn back to Gabriek.

Lots of people are watching, but I don't care. I give him a hug.

'See you in Australia,' I say.

'I'm proud of you, Felix,' he says.

We hug for a few more moments, then Gabriek steps back several paces. Which is typical of how thoughtful he is. When it's this hard to say goodbye, having a bit of space helps.

I give Celeste a hug as well.

'Thank you for saving us too,' I say to her.

'No thanks needed,' she says. 'You're repaying me a hundred times. And don't worry about Anya. You'll see her again.'

'And you'll see your mum again,' I say, patting the pocket of my flying suit where I've got my few precious things and Celeste's letter to her mother.

'I've got your mail safe too,' says Celeste. 'I'll post them today. It's really sweet of you, Felix, sending farewell letters to your old neighbours in the city.'

I nod gratefully.

Best not to go into any explanations.

Celeste and Gabriek would only worry if I told them how those letters are going to save them all from Zliv.

I get on the plane.

Maybe everybody feels scared when they fly for the first time.

Even before they've taken off.

I think they must do because Simmo is being very understanding.

'We've given you the double room,' he says as he gets me settled into my turret.

He's joking.

We're in a four-engined bomber the size of a castle, but this turret is tiny. Probably because it's under the front of the plane and if it was any bigger it would scrape on the runway.

'Don't worry,' I say. 'This is bigger than the hole I lived in once.'

Simmo gives me a look.

I hope I haven't insulted his plane. I tell him I really like this turret, specially the perspex walls.

'Great view from here,' I say. 'And it's good you and Rusty are just up there in the cockpit. In the barn I had Dom just above my head. He was a very kind horse but he used to stamp a lot.'

Simmo gives me another look.

It's a sympathetic one.

While he shows me how to buckle myself in and use the intercom in my flying helmet and get oxygen through my face mask, he also tells me what he thinks of Nazis and the things they did to children.

'Mongrels,' he says.

Then he goes back up to the cockpit and one by one the engines clatter and start to roar.

'Righty-ho,' says Rusty's voice in my helmet. 'Relax and enjoy the flight, Felix. Best spot in the plane you've got there.'

'Thanks,' I say, trying not to sound too nervous.

Suddenly the engines go from a small roar to a big roar and we lurch forward along the runway.

This is fast.

I thought Celeste driving the truck was fast, but this is very fast.

'Ever been up in a crate?' yells Rusty's voice.

I'm not sure what a crate is, but the highest up I've ever been is an orphanage in the mountains, so I say no.

'Hang on,' says Rusty. 'Up we go.'

I close my eyes. Everything is rattling. I hope Simmo the flight engineer isn't up the back playing cards with Ken, which Ken invited him to do. I hope he's in the cockpit with a spanner tightening things.

I open my eyes.

And gape.

Through the perspex walls, everything is getting small very quickly. Far below, the air base looks like a breadboard with a few caraway seeds on it, which are probably people.

I wave in case Gabriek and Celeste can see me.

Maybe even Anya.

The farms down there look like the checked eiderdown that Mum and Dad used to have on their bed. They cuddled me on it a lot.

'Good view, eh?' says Rusty's voice. 'I'll fly under the clouds for as long as I can so you can see the sights.'

'Thank you,' I say.

I stare through the perspex for ages.

It's all there. My whole life.

Getting smaller and smaller.

I can't actually see everything, all the places and all the people I've been lucky to have, but I can see them in my imagination.

The orphanage. The cellar. The farm. The forest. All the places that have given me good protection.

Mum, Dad, Zelda, Barney, Genia, Doctor Zajak, Yuli, Celeste, Gabriek, Anya. Everyone I've cared about. Everyone I've lost.

And now I'm leaving them all behind.

'Goodbye,' I whisper.

I let my sad thoughts gently touch them all for a while.

Then I realise something.

Oops.

All the flight crew up here would have heard me saying goodbye in their helmets. And it's probably one of the few Polish words they understand.

But nobody has said anything. They know it was a private moment.

I like Australians.

We're flying over a big city.

It looks big enough to be the city where me and Gabriek and Anya used to live. I wonder if Zliv is there, looking up at this plane and wondering.

No. Why would he?

He hasn't got my letter yet.

The plane gives a lurch.

'Whoa,' says Rusty's voice. 'That flap's a bit sticky. Have to look at that when we refuel.'

'Will do,' says Simmo's voice.

'Felix,' says Rusty. 'If there's anything you want to know about Australia, just ask.'

'Thanks,' I say. 'Is it true about the universities? That they're very good?'

Rusty doesn't reply.

For a moment I think he's busy trying to deal with the sticky flap, but then I hear him blowing air into his mask like people do when they don't know an answer.

Simmo answers instead.

'Mine was great,' he says. 'University of life.'

Wally's voice breaks in.

'My cousin went to a technical college,' he says. 'She reckoned the canteen was good.'

'What about the police in Australia?' I say. 'Are they good?'

'Definitely,' says Rusty. 'Best in the world.'

'Very tough,' says Simmo. 'But fair.'

That's a relief to hear.

'Thanks,' I say.

I don't ask for further details. Such as how well-trained and well-equipped the Australian police are. And whether they'd be able to deal with a ruthless fanatical Polish killer coming to Australia on a tip-off.

If they can't, it's too late now.

This Lancaster is very comfortable for a warplane that was built for bombing, not sleeping.

I closed my eyes about half an hour ago for a nap and dropped straight off. Must be the steady drone of the engines and the gentle vibration. The whole plane sort of rocks you to sleep.

Wait a minute.

It's dark. It was daylight when we took off.

I try to stand up.

Then I remember I'm plugged in and hooked up to oxygen and other important things.

'Hello,' I say into the intercom.

I hope the others aren't all asleep too. It's starting to feel lonely down here.

I shiver because I've just realised what this turret was probably used for. Aiming large numbers of bombs at people and cows.

'Felix is awake,' says Simmo's voice.

'Yes I am,' I say, relieved.

'You know how to sleep,' says Ken's voice. 'Been out for hours. I was going to wake you when we landed in Beirut to refuel, but the others said to let you be.'

Landed?

How did I sleep through a landing?

I realise what's happened. It's the travel sickness pills that the supervising medical officer gave me. I took a couple earlier in case the flight got bumpy. They must be sleeping pills as well.

'Where are we now?' I say.

'Dunno exactly,' says Ken. 'On our way to India.'

'We're over Saudi Arabia,' says another voice, which must be Gav the navigator.

'You hungry, young fella?' says Simmo's voice. 'You missed your meal in Beirut. No problem, we've got rations. Fancy some dried beef?'

'Thanks,' I say.

I've never had dried beef, but it can't be that different from beef that's still a bit damp.

'I'll get him a feed,' says Simmo.

'Rations are in the kitbags,' says Rusty's voice. 'Rear turret.'

It's very thoughtful of them. I am hungry. But there's something else gnawing at my tummy.

With all the rushing around before we left Poland, and all the sleeping since, I haven't had a chance to check something with Ken.

'Ken,' I say. 'What did the base commander say about medical backup for Anya when she has the baby?'

The intercom is silent for a while.

'We had a good conversation,' says Ken's voice eventually. 'It went well. Very well.'

I don't say anything. I wait for details.

'As I predicted earlier,' says Ken, 'the commander wasn't specifically prepared to authorise the birth of a baby at the base hospital. But he did offer to arrange something else. Just as good, if not better.'

I don't believe it.

I struggle not to get furious. Being furious might use up too much oxygen.

It's no good, I am furious.

We had a deal.

I'm on this plane because we had a deal. And now Ken is telling me, when we're halfway to India, that the deal is off.

'What something else?' I say. 'What is it that's just as good, if not better?'

I have a horrible feeling I know.

'A very good charity,' says Ken. 'One that's totally kitted out for babies. Hundreds are born in their excellent hospitals every month.'

I knew it.

I want to scream.

I want to go up into the fuselage and place my hands round Ken's neck and squeeze it very hard. I want to make Rusty turn this crate around, now.

Anya and I talked about charities months ago. We made enquiries to see if any of them would be a good place to have a baby. And we decided that for a person of Anya's age, definitely not.

For one very good reason.

If you're under eighteen, charities take your baby away. They have it adopted. No choice. You never see your baby again.

'Felix,' says Ken.

He can probably tell how upset I am from my heavy breathing on the intercom.

'It's not that bad,' he says.

I'm speechless. How does a person this stupid get a job this important?

Simmo must have plugged his helmet back in at the rear of the plane because I hear him give a puzzled grunt.

'Weird,' he says. 'There's definitely dried beef here somewhere.'

I hear him undoing a kitbag.

And giving another grunt.

'This doesn't feel like dried beef,' he says.

Another voice replies, muffled. I can't make out what it's saying, but I can tell it's angry.

'Jeez,' says Simmo, sounding very alarmed.

There's a confusion of voices, all alarmed, all speaking at once.

Then Wally's voice breaks through.

'Rusty,' he yells. 'There's someone here hiding in a bag. Can't see who it is, but they've got a gun and they're pointing it at Simmo's head.'

The plane gives a wobble, then straightens up.

'Everyone stay calm,' says Rusty's voice.

He doesn't sound calm.

My insides have gone weak. Just as well I've got a urine bottle tucked inside this flying suit.

Did Zliv find out I was going to Australia even before I sent the letter? Did he stow away on the plane?

'Don't,' yells Simmo's voice. 'Don't shoot.'

'I won't,' says another voice. 'But only if you remove your very rude hands.'

My insides go even weaker.

It's Anya.

Maybe Ken will calm down soon.

Stop panicking about what his bosses in the Australian government will say. See that Anya needs his help, not his bad temper.

Anya has tried to explain several times.

'What other choice did I have?' she said to Ken. 'I had to get away. The stupid base commander told some charity where I was. The charity is probably at Celeste's right now, tearing up the floorboards looking for me. Once charities decide to help you, they never give up till they find you.'

I'm very proud of her.

She's risked everything for her baby, which I think Australians will admire.

Ken isn't convinced.

'The Australian people,' he yells at Anya, 'will have no sympathy at all for a girl with a baby and a gun.'

I think he's wrong.

They'll love her.

Except maybe the gun.

Ken is even worse now we've landed in India. I think it's the heat. He's leaning against an oil drum on the tarmac, glaring at Anya.

'I should have you arrested,' he growls. 'Thrown in a local jail and left to rot.'

'No,' I say. 'You can't do that.'

If he makes Anya leave the plane here in India, she's finished. A sixteen-year-old girl having a baby in a foreign prison wouldn't stand a chance. The prison guards probably don't even know what a placenta is, or a cervix.

I can see that the crew agree with me.

Well, Rusty and Gav and Wally do. They've stopped chewing their chicken and are giving Ken unhappy looks. I think Simmo would agree as well if he wasn't up a ladder with a couple of Indian mechanics fixing the wing flap.

'Before I decide, young lady,' says Ken with a scowl, 'your best hope is to tell me who helped you. A kid like you doesn't kit yourself out with a flying suit and an oxygen tank and then smuggle yourself onto a plane, not all on your own.'

Ken clearly doesn't know Anya.

But instead of saying that nobody helped her, Anya just shakes her head.

'I don't rat on my friends,' she says in Polish.

I hope Ken didn't understand that. Because it sounds like Celeste and Dougie must have helped.

Probably Gabriek too. The three of them will be in big trouble if anyone finds out.

I change the subject to get the pressure off Anya.

'Let's eat our food,' I say to Ken. 'It'll get cold.'

Ken gives me a scathing look.

'Looks like good tucker,' Simmo calls down to Ken from the ladder.

I think he's trying to get the pressure off Anya too. Which is kind, seeing he's still got a small pink circle on his forehead from Anya's gun barrel.

'Best chicken in brown sauce I've ever tasted,' says Wally, also trying to help.

I'm too stressed to eat.

So is Anya.

'One day you'll understand,' she says to Ken. 'You'll be sick of people taking things from you. You'll decide that just once in your life you're going to keep something that's yours.'

Ken scowls at her.

'There's only one thing I'd like to keep,' he says, speaking very slowly as if he wants every word to hurt Anya. 'I'd like to keep the very large amount of cash we could have pocketed if we'd wanted an extra passenger. Europe's full of people who'll pay anything to get away. Nazis, criminals, politicians, all kinds of cashed-up desperados. And what have we got instead? A freeloader. A parasite.'

Anya glares at him.

We both know that word, parasite. It's in the hygiene section of the baby book.

I know how that must hurt Anya.

She's taken care of herself since she was a little kid. She's always paid her way, even if she did have to borrow a bit from shops and armies without them realising it.

Rusty is giving Ken a hard look too.

'Not,' says Rusty, 'that we'd ever take a cashed-up desperado. Not if we had a choice between that and a mother protecting her baby.'

Ken glares at Rusty then stands up as if he's made a decision.

'There must be a Polish Consul in India,' he says. 'We'll leave our illegal stowaway with the local police. They can contact the Polish Consul and he can take over the whole mess.'

I stand up too.

'If you leave Anya here,' I say to Ken, 'you'll leave me as well.'

Ken glowers.

'And what if I don't want to?' he says. 'What if I make you get back on the plane?'

'You won't be able to,' I say, trying to stop my voice wobbling. 'I was trained by partisans.'

'And I have friends in the Indian army,' snarls Ken. 'One phone call, that's all it would take.'

Rusty and Gav and Wally have stopped eating again. They look like they're in shock.

'If you do,' I say, 'I'll tell the Australian people about my most horrible and terrible experience. The time a dear friend of mine, an innocent child violated by war, was abandoned by an employee of the Australian government thousands of miles from home.'

'Yeah,' mutters Wally. 'We'll tell them that too.'

'I'm not a child,' says Anya. 'But thanks.'

'All fixed,' yells Simmo from up the ladder. 'All ready to go.'

Ken glares across the runway into the heat haze as if he's hoping there's another young European war survivor blowing around out there among the dust spirals.

There isn't.

'Back on the plane,' he snaps.

'Thank you, Ken,' says Anya.

He turns to her, furious.

'Not another word from you,' he says. 'Not one squeak for the rest of the flight.'

'Ken,' I say. 'Anya will be wonderful in Australia. We can keep her gun out of sight and she'll win everyone's heart. Australians love babies. You told us yourself the Australian government wants all the population it can get.'

Ken scowls at me.

'If you want to get to Australia in one piece,' he says, 'you'll keep your trap shut too.'

As he storms off, Anya turns to me, grinning, and makes a motion of buttoning her lip.

I smile back, then turn away.

Another grateful look from Anya is more than I can deal with right now.

I've got too much to do.

Pluck up the courage, mostly, to tell Anya the main reason I was too stressed to eat.

To tell her that while Australia has wonderful hospitals, and her baby will be born in the safest possible way, I've done something that could put them both in terrible danger.

'Maybe,' says Anya, 'the reason these stars are so clear and bright is because the air in Australia doesn't have much bomb dust in it.'

We're in the upper gun turret and she's gazing out through the perspex dome, happier than I've ever seen her. Which makes me feel even more desperate and miserable.

I'm such a coward. All the hours and all the refuelling stops since Bombay, and I still haven't told her.

'Hurry up sunrise,' says Anya, peering into the darkness whizzing past below us. 'If Australia is as beautiful as its stars, I can't wait to see it.'

I sigh.

I should be feeling as happy as she is. Snuggled up in our private place on top of the plane. Our shoulders pressed together. Sharing an oxygen cylinder. Warmed by the gentle breeze from the heating tube Simmo rigged up for us.

This should be the happiest night of my life.

But it's not.

'Anya,' I say in a shaky voice. 'There's something I have to tell you.'

She looks at me.

We're only using our breathing masks when we need them, and there's enough moonlight for me to see the little smile on her face.

Oh no. She thinks I'm going to say something romantic.

'I have to confess something,' I say.

She's still smiling.

Surely there's enough moonlight for Anya to see the look on my face, which I'm pretty sure isn't romantic. I'm pretty sure it's anxious and miserable. So why can't she see?

She does.

She's not smiling now.

'What?' she says.

I reach into the pocket of my flying suit and take out the piece of paper I've been trying to be brave enough to show her since we left Bombay. The copy of the letter I wrote in Poland.

'This letter,' I say. 'I sent it to some of our old neighbours in the city. I figured that at least one of them would be able to get it to the person it's actually written to.'

I don't say any more. I just let her read it. I know it off by heart, so I don't look at the words, just Anya's face.

Dear Zliv,
It's me you want, not Gabriek or Anya.
I caused your brother's death, just me.
But you'll have to come to Australia to
kill me, because that's where I'm going.
If you don't believe me, check the
Australian newspapers.
Felix.

Anya stares at me.

I know what she's going to say.

That I shouldn't have written the letter. That it was a crazy idea.

But she doesn't say that.

'Felix,' she says, exasperated. 'How can Zliv check Australian newspapers in Poland?'

I've thought about this.

'The city library,' I say.

'The last time I looked,' says Anya, 'the library didn't have any newspapers. Just rats.'

I've thought about that too. It's true this plan does partly depend on Polish libraries being fixed up very quickly.

The plane gives a sudden jolt.

A big one.

We both glance through the perspex.

That's strange. The stars have vanished. For a second I don't get it. Then I realise they must be behind clouds.

'Zliv can look at Polish newspapers too,' I say.

'Ken said he was sending the photos he took of me at the air base to the Polish press as well.'

The plane jolts again.

A storm.

From Anya's face when I showed her the letter, I think there's a storm inside her too.

'I'm sorry I put you and the baby in danger,' I say.

Anya looks at me.

'You were trying to protect us,' she says.

She kisses me on the cheek.

A searing flash of white light leaves my eyeballs blurred and tingling. When my vision clears, I see Anya rubbing her eyes too.

'Lightning,' says Anya. 'That was close.'

Thunder rumbles all around us.

I can hear a different sound coming from the plane engines. As if they're working harder. And a whining sound. As if some other part of the plane isn't working properly.

At our last refuelling stop, Rusty explained what a pilot does with storms. Tries to fly around them.

The plane gives another big jolt. Several of them.

I don't think we're flying around this storm.

'Let's not worry, Felix,' says Anya. 'Zliv probably won't come to Australia.'

I know she's trying to make me feel better, but the thought of that makes me feel even worse.

Zliv and Gabriek both in Poland. Zliv deciding that killing Gabriek is better than nothing.

No, he has to come.

I think he will. Flying to Australia is much easier than swimming across the Danube in winter.

Anya is reaching into her flying suit. It's too big for her so the cuffs are rolled up, which makes it hard to get her hand into the pocket.

But she does, and pulls out her gun.

'If he does come,' she says, 'we'll deal with him. You and me.'

'And the Australian police,' I say.

Anya doesn't hear me because of another huge crash of thunder.

'Everything will be fine,' she says after it stops.

She squeezes my hand.

There's an explosion that leaves my ears ringing. White light even brighter than before. Except this time it doesn't disappear, it stays all around us.

Everywhere. All over the plane.

White fire dancing.

'Don't touch anything,' yells Anya. 'I think we've been struck by lightning.'

Below us on one wing there's suddenly fire of a different colour. Yellow and red flames, pouring out of both engines.

'We've got to tell the others,' I say.

We scramble frantically down from the turret into the fuselage.

Where I see that the others don't need telling. They know. The stink of the burning engines is filling the plane. And the noise of screaming machinery and the yells of panicking men.

Simmo grabs us.

'Get these on,' he shouts.

He forces backpacks over our heads and straps them on. Round our tummies and round our legs. Which makes me realise they're not backpacks.

They're parachutes.

'We're going down,' yells Simmo. 'The fuel valves are jammed. I can't extinguish the engines. Rusty will try a hard landing, but it might be too hard. So you've got a choice.'

I don't understand a couple of the words, but I know what the choice is.

I've faced a choice like this before.

Ken is kneeling on the fuselage floor, shaking his head, staring in terror at the parachute pack in his hands.

'You can stay,' shouts Simmo to me and Anya, 'or you can jump.'

I look at Anya.

I try to let her see I've done this before. That sometimes the scariest choice is the best.

Behind us Simmo starts kicking at something with the heel of his boot. Something on the wall of the fuselage. Suddenly a section of the wall flies away into the night sky.

Outside, darkness screams past the hole.

Anya doesn't flinch.

'I'll do what you do,' she says.

'After you've jumped,' yells Simmo, 'count to ten, then pull the cord.'

He stuffs a length of cord into each of our hands.

Anya's eyes are still on me, not wavering.

I take her hand.

When I was ten, I had this choice. On a train to a Nazi death camp. Stay or jump. There were machine guns outside, and darkness. I was holding the hand of a friend then as well.

We survived.

'No,' whimpers Ken.

I look at Anya one more time, and we jump.

Maybe Anya is behind me.

I peer through the ropes of my parachute into the blackness of the night sky.

Nothing.

I can't see her above me, or below. I'm alone, floating down through dark emptiness.

'Anya,' I yell.

No reply. Even the wind has gone silent.

All I can hear is the dying howl of the plane somewhere in the distance.

I had to let go of Anya's hand. I didn't want to but I had to. As we jumped, Simmo yelled at me to let go. For a second I didn't understand why.

Then it hit me at the same time as the rush of air outside the plane. If I didn't let go of Anya's hand, we'd be too close when we finished counting to ten. When we pulled our cords, our parachutes would get tangled up together.

Being too close would kill us.

So I let go and she was swept away.

'Anya,' I yell again.

The only sound in reply is one I don't want to hear. A distant explosion. The plane making its hard landing.

Very hard.

I don't want to look, but I do.

Oh.

Way down there, far off to one side, who knows how many miles away, tiny balls of flame.

I think of Simmo, more concerned about us than himself.

And Ken, too scared to jump.

I hope the plane was empty when it hit the ground. I hope Simmo and Rusty and the others got to choose a soft landing. I hope their parachutes are out there somewhere in the darkness.

'Simmo,' I yell.

I look around again, but I can't see any of them.

What I can see is something incredible.

A thin crack of light opening up in front of me. From one side of my vision to the other. The crack is so long I can't see where it starts or ends. The whole dark world splitting in two.

Have I got concussion again?

When my parachute opened, did the sickening jolt snap something in my brain stem?

Slowly the crack starts to change shape. Becomes a hazy glow. As if light is spilling over the edge of something.

Which it is. The orange rim of the sun appears over the edge of a huge horizon, throwing shadows across a vast landscape.

I feel so weak with relief that if my legs weren't dangling in space, I'm pretty sure they wouldn't hold me up.

It's not concussion, it's Australia.

'Anya,' I yell desperately into the fuzzy sparkling air all around me. 'Simmo.'

Six parachutes, that's what I want to see.

But I can only see one. And it's too far away to tell if hanging from the ropes is a precious pregnant person, or an engineer, or a pilot, or a terrified employee of the Australian government.

What I can see is Australia.

Below me.

Everywhere.

It's huge. The beams of sunlight go on forever.

I stare at Australia between my feet, and realise something scary.

Australia is getting closer.

Very fast.

Sometimes it's good to have weak legs.

They buckle when you hit the ground and you don't crack your pelvic skeletal structure and shatter your coccyx.

It's also good to have strong glasses that fit tightly. Thanks air-base staff. I hope there are kind people like you in this part of the world.

I crawl out from under the parachute cloth and undo the straps.

Then I look around for Anya.

I force myself to concentrate on another good thing. The possibility that she's still alive.

I can't see her. All I can see is flat dusty ground with spindly bushes. And beyond that, more flat dusty ground with more spindly bushes. And, not too far away, one small hill.

I head for it.

As I plod over the flat dusty ground, I'm grateful the storm didn't include rain. This would be a lake of mud after rain. Which is the last thing you need when you're trying to find your special person in a new country.

I scramble up the rocky hill.

At the top I peer around. You'd think I'd see her. A parachute isn't small. The amount of cloth must be about the same as five hundred pairs of underpants. You'd think even from this distance you'd see five hundred pairs of underpants lying on the ground.

I don't see anything lying on the ground.

No parachute, no Anya.

I have a horrible thought. Anya hasn't got weak legs. I've seen her leg muscles. They wouldn't have buckled when she hit the ground. What if she's lying out there somewhere, half covered in dust with a shattered pelvic skeletal structure and a badly damaged tummy . . .

I don't want to think about it.

I need something to attract Anya's attention, even if she's only half-conscious. Something that can reflect sunlight.

I think of just the thing. I reach into my flight-suit pocket and find it.

Cyryl Szynsky's gold ring.

I give it a rub and hold it up in the rays of the dawn sun and twist it around so it gleams.

I'm worried the gleam isn't bright enough, so I do it for a long time.

'Anya,' I yell, over and over.

I'm still doing it when suddenly, not far in the distance, a gleaming red ball shoots up into the sky and hangs there.

A flare.

The flare has burnt out when I arrive at the place where I saw it.

Where I think I saw it.

But I still can't see Anya.

All I can see are more spindly bushes. All I can hear are the very strange Australian birds.

I start to yell Anya's name again, then stop.

In Poland, when you're somewhere unfamiliar, you don't go around yelling out loud so everyone knows you're there. Not until you've worked out if it's a safe place.

Is Australia a safe place?

Rusty and Simmo made it sound safe.

I open my mouth to call to Anya. Before I can, somebody grabs me from behind.

A gunshot explodes so close I almost need the urine bottle again.

Somebody appears from behind me. I'm so dazed I take a moment to realise it's Anya.

She points to the ground near my feet. In the dust is a snake. Blood is dribbling from where its head should be.

'That was close,' says Anya, her voice shaky.

I can't speak. Too much shock. Too much relief that Anya's OK.

She gives me a hug.

'We made it,' she says.

'Yes,' I croak.

Because we've both still got our flying suits on, it's hard to get our arms all the way around each other. So we hug extra tight with what we've got.

Then Anya pulls away.

'Mustn't squash the baby,' she says.

'Are you alright?' I say. 'Your legs? Your pelvic structure?'

'They're fine,' says Anya. 'I've just got a few scratches. From the dry bushes I landed on.'

She doesn't look alright. She looks badly shaken up. I should have noticed that before, instead of getting carried away hugging her.

I take a deep breath and try to focus, like Doctor Zajak taught me.

'I should examine you,' I say. 'Parachute jumps

aren't good for unborn babies, medically speaking.'

Anya looks at me doubtfully.

'Lie down on your parachute,' I say. 'Just a quick check.'

'I buried my parachute,' she says.

I look at her, surprised.

'That's what you do with parachutes,' she says. 'I read about it.'

Before she met me, Anya hadn't read many books. It's good she's catching up now.

'The ground's soft,' I say. 'It's mostly dust.'

We check the ground for more snakes. Then Anya lies down on a soft patch.

She empties the pockets of her flying suit.

Several packets of dried beef. Her gun. The baby book. A flare pistol.

'I'll leave my flying suit on,' she says.

Carefully I feel her tummy with both hands.

I'm not sure exactly how to do this because I haven't got up to abdominal examinations in the baby book. I don't want to refer to it now in front of her, so I go as gently as I can.

'Where did you get the flare gun?' I say.

I've read how it's good for doctors to start a conversation while they're doing something that might make patients feel a bit embarrassed.

'I stole it from the plane,' says Anya.

I feel something moving under my hands.

'The baby kicks sometimes,' says Anya. 'Specially after parachute jumps.'

I nod. It's all I can do. I'm feeling a bit emotional at meeting Anya's baby for the first time.

As far as I can tell, the baby feels alive and healthy.

'Felix,' says Anya quietly. 'The others didn't make it, did they?'

I don't know what to say.

If possible, expectant mothers shouldn't get too upset. Nor should their doctors.

'I saw it,' says Anya. 'The plane crashing and exploding. And I didn't see any other parachutes.'

'Doesn't mean there weren't any,' I say, glancing up at the sky. 'Let's be hopeful.'

'I'd rather be hopeful about the house,' says Anya.

I stare at her.

'House?' I say. 'What house?'

Maybe even if the people in this house are unkind and chase us away, they'll give us a glass of water first.

I croak this to Anya.

She looks at me.

'You're thinking about bad things again,' she says. 'The people here might be nice.'

She's right. I'm slipping back into old habits. I think I'm suffering from heat exhaustion and possibly dehydration of the brain.

It's taken us hours to walk here. We're parched. But only a couple of fields to go, dry and dusty ones with a few spindly cattle in them.

And then the house. If we don't faint first.

I see something up ahead. I put my arm round Anya and help her towards it.

A rusty cattle trough with muddy water in it.

We drop to our knees and drink, gulping the water, not caring about the mud.

As soon as my thirst goes, I feel starving.

Anya does too. She pulls slices of dried beef out of her pocket and we stuff them into our mouths. Then we try to brush some of the dust off ourselves and smooth our sweaty hair.

'I still can't believe it,' I say. 'Why didn't I see this house on the way down?'

'There's only the one,' says Anya. 'So it was easy to miss.'

That's one of the reasons I like Anya so much. She's kind. A lot of people aren't these days.

'Have we got our story straight?' I say to her.

We rehearse it one more time, then we walk through the last fields to the house.

There's a battered old truck parked next to the house, which I'm glad to see. Somebody must be home.

There are two front doors.

The first one is a strange wire-mesh door, swinging loose. I open it and knock on the main door behind it. Both doors are as battered and old as the truck and as dry and dusty as the rest of the house and the rest of Australia.

Nobody comes.

I knock a few more times, then yell 'hello' a few times as loudly as I can.

No reply.

'Must be out,' I say.

We look around at the fields. Nobody working there. Where could the people be? There are no neighbours to pop over to for a game of cards or to borrow a hose to wash the house.

'We'll have to take the truck,' says Anya.

I look at her.

'We haven't got a key,' I say.

Anya rolls her eyes. I forget sometimes she used to have her own crime gang in the city.

As Anya moves towards the truck, the door of the house swings open.

An elderly man with white hair and a stubbly beard stares at us.

'What?' he says.

I hesitate for a moment, partly because the man looks angry and partly to get our story straight in my head.

'Hello, sir,' I say in my best English. 'Can you help us please? We were camping nearby and the storm blew our tent away.'

The man doesn't say anything. Just stares at me and Anya like he can't believe what he's seeing.

I don't blame him.

We probably do look a bit strange. We decided to leave our flying suits on. One of the English books our neighbour lent us was about the Bedouins, and how Bedouin people always wear thick clothes in the desert. They think it's better to be a bit sweaty than sunburned to death.

Before we set off this morning, I managed to smash a small rock into a sort of blade and trim the arms and legs of our flying suits down to size.

We twisted the chopped-off pieces of cloth together to make hats.

'We were wondering, sir,' I say to the man, snatching my hat off my head, which I meant to do before I knocked, 'if you could please give us a lift to the nearest town?'

The man still doesn't say anything.

Just stares.

Which I think is a bit rude. OK, our clothes are covered in dust, but it's not as if he's a very stylish dresser himself. His clothes are baggy and they look like he's slept in them.

'Please,' says Anya.

'Camping?' says the man.

I nod.

'Don't talk rubbish,' says the man. 'Nobody goes camping around here.'

Anya and I glance at each other.

I knew this would be risky, telling lies in a new country. But we can't tell the truth. 'Hello, sir, we just parachuted in.' He wouldn't believe us.

'I reckon,' says the man, peering more closely at our clothes, 'that you two must have bailed out of that plane that went down this morning.'

I stare at him, stunned.

Anya does too.

'I spent most of the war in Darwin,' says the man. 'Japs bombed us a few times, but they didn't always get away with it. When you've heard a damaged plane going down, you never forget the sound.'

I'm barely taking in what he's saying.

'Well?' says the man. 'Am I right?'

Suddenly I haven't got the strength to tell any more lies.

I nod.

The man gives us a sympathetic smile.

'Why didn't you say so,' he says. 'You've had a rough day, wandering around in the scrub in that clobber. Feeling a bit sad probably about the poor bloke who was flying the plane. I reckon you two need a cuppa. Come in.'

That was the most delicious pot of tea and pile of toasted cheese sandwiches I've ever had.

'Good?' said Jack as we ate.

I nodded gratefully.

'If I do say so myself,' said Jack, 'I make a tiptop toasted sanger.'

I'm learning quite a lot of Australian now.

Being allowed to wash our hands and faces in Jack's kitchen was pretty tiptop too. But the best thing is that Jack is so friendly.

'I reckon,' says Jack, as we bump along in his truck, the three of us squeezed in the front, 'that what you both need are some new clothes. Which is why I'm taking you to Mrs Tingwell's shop.'

I glance at Anya.

She's a bit concerned by this, just like I am.

'That's very kind, Jack,' she says, 'but we don't have any money.'

'No problem,' says Jack. 'This is drought country. Nobody's got any money. Mrs T does credit.'

I'm not sure exactly what that means, but when Jack says no problem he sounds like he means it.

While we were having tea, Jack asked me and Anya about our life stories. We didn't tell him much, because it's rude to only talk about yourself when you visit someone. But we told him a bit.

Jack's a person who chuckles quite a lot, but a couple of times while I was telling him about what happened to Mum and Dad and Zelda and Genia, he wiped away tears.

And when Anya mentioned the Russian soldier who made her pregnant, Jack got angry, but in a way that showed he didn't blame her at all.

Which I thought was very kind.

'Nearly there,' says Jack as we bump along the dirt road. 'Only a couple of hours to go.'

I'm peering at the horizon, wondering where Simmo and Rusty and the others have ended up.

Jack sees me squinting into the distance.

'Felix,' he says. 'Fraid it's not looking good for your mates. I reckon that plane went down in the high country. Very remote, lot of sheer rock, no way an ambulance could even get up there. Anyone on board when that plane ploughed the paddock wouldn't have had a chance.'

I don't understand every word of this, but I get the gist from the sad look on Jack's face and the way he gives my shoulder a sympathetic squeeze.

'Maybe they all jumped,' I say. 'They all had their parachutes. They were all experts.'

'Felix,' says Anya softly. 'The plane was in a death dive. I don't think counting to ten and not holding hands would have been enough.'

I don't say anything.

She's probably right.

But everyone has to accept things in their own time, that's what Mother Minka taught me in the orphanage.

Jack is giving me a look.

'Everything you've copped in your life,' he says, 'and you're still up for giving hope a go. I reckon there's a few individuals in these parts could learn from that. Good on you, young fella.'

'Thank you,' I say.

'Anyhow,' says Jack, 'most of all, I'm glad the three of you made it.'

Anya gives Jack one of her grateful looks, and his steering goes wobbly for a moment.

I hope all the Aussies we meet are like Jack.

Because if they are, even if poor Ken didn't make it, our trip can still be a success. The Australian government can get someone else to take over. We can still meet lots of people and help them feel better about the war. And we can still be in all the newspapers, including the Polish ones.

So by the time Gabriek and Celeste arrive on the first boat, and we take Celeste to see her mum, things can be tiptop.

Anya will have had her baby somewhere very friendly and safe.

We'll have sorted out all our problems.

Even, with the help of the Australian police, the biggest one.

Maybe Jack hasn't seen Mrs Tingwell for a while. Maybe since he last saw her, she's developed a painful medical condition. One that's made her stop being the friendly and generous person Jack described. One that makes her scowl a lot.

Boils in the rectal passage, something like that.

Poor lady.

'What's this, Jack Duggan?' says Mrs Tingwell, scowling at me and Anya. 'What trouble have you brought me today?'

Even with a medical condition, you'd think Mrs Tingwell would be more cheerful than that.

Her shop is huge.

It's more like a Polish department store, but without the rubble. It's got the same iron pillars as in Poland, holding up two levels of balconies full of clothes and customers. And it's right on the main street of the town, so it's not like she has to spend a fortune on advertisements.

Jack touches the brim of his hat to Mrs Tingwell.

'Couple of waifs from war-devastated Europe,' he says. 'Bailed out of that plane that went down last night.'

'Hello,' I say to Mrs Tingwell and the customers in my best English. 'We're very happy to be in your friendly country.'

The customers are gathering around, inspecting me and Anya suspiciously.

Specially Anya.

I can see she's starting to look uncomfortable.

I hope she remembers what I mentioned to her about the gun in her pocket. How it's best not to get it out while we're shopping.

'Any news?' says Jack to the customers. 'About the plane?'

Most of them shake their heads.

'Terrible,' says one man.

'I heard it was the Japs,' says a woman. 'Having a last crack at us.'

Jack gives her a look.

'War's been over for a year, Mrs Gleeson,' he says. He nods towards me and Anya. 'These aren't Japs.'

Mrs Tingwell is staring at Anya's tummy.

Anya's flying suit is too large for her but you can still see the bulge. I wish Anya hadn't left her big coat on the plane.

'Is that child expecting?' says Mrs Tingwell.

'I am not a child,' mutters Anya.

'She is pregnant, yes,' says Jack.

The customers look shocked. A couple of them say things under their breath.

'Disgusting,' says Mrs Tingwell to Anya's tummy. She glares at me. 'Is he the father?'

'No,' I say indignantly.

Anya looks hurt.

'I'm not the father scientifically speaking,' I say to Mrs Tingwell, 'but I will be giving the child lots of love.'

Anya smiles at me.

Jack explains to the customers about the Russian soldier. They look even more shocked, but a few of them look sympathetic as well.

'And you believe that story, Jack Duggan?' says a man wearing expensive-looking riding boots.

'Yes, I do,' says Jack, giving the man a fierce look. 'I wouldn't have said it if I didn't.'

'I think you're out of your depth,' says the man. 'The Russian communists are grabbing power in Europe and we know they're trying to worm their way in here. Just how much do you know about these two individuals?'

Jack rolls his eyes.

'Grow up, Carson,' he says to the man. 'These two war orphans are not communists.'

Mrs Tingwell snorts.

'If the commos wanted to win us over,' she says, 'these are exactly the types they'd send.'

The man in the riding boots comes closer to me and Anya.

'You two,' he says. 'Do you believe we should share everything equally?'

He speaks very loudly as if he thinks we're stupid. Well, I'm not stupid. I've learned my lesson about telling lies in a new country. And this man obviously doesn't believe in sharing equally. His boots would have cost more than all the other boots in this place put together.

'Yes,' I say. 'I do believe in sharing.'

The man nods grimly, like he was hoping I'd say that. Well let him gloat if he thinks he's won. I'm glad I told the truth.

One of the shop assistants, a girl about Anya's age, hurries over.

'I've called the police,' she says to Mrs Tingwell. She looks at me guiltily. 'Sorry,' she says.

Jack looks alarmed.

He pulls out a battered old wallet, takes out some money and pushes the notes into my hand.

'Me and the police don't get on too well,' he mutters to me. 'And given the mood here, I don't think we'll ask for credit.'

He gives my shoulder a squeeze and takes one of Anya's hands and kisses it.

He turns to Mrs Tingwell.

'These customers would like a well-made shirt and trousers,' he says, 'and a baggy frock.'

Then he hurries out of the shop. A few moments later we hear his truck starting up and driving away.

Mrs Tingwell grabs the money out of my hand.

'Don't be too choosy,' she says. 'You haven't got long. The police station's only two doors away.'

This cell is cold.

I think it's because the sun's gone down and it's so damp in here.

I rub my bare arms.

What a crazy country. Scorching one moment, freezing the next. With a large clothing emporium that didn't have a single garment in our sizes with long sleeves. And a police force that locks people up just because they're foreign.

For a few moments I miss Gabriek so much that my cardiovascular system hurts.

I just wish I could tell him how crazy Australia is and how I'm already having doubts about the Australian police force.

But that would only make him worry.

Stop it, I tell myself. Gabriek's not here. You're the one who has to fix this.

'Any ideas?' whispers Anya next to me on the wooden bench.

'I'm still thinking,' I say.

Anya is shivering in her short-sleeved baggy frock. If we weren't both in full view of the police officers, I'd give her a hug to warm her up.

Instead I go over to the cell bars.

'Excuse me,' I say to the police officers. 'When can we have our flying suits back?'

'You can't,' says one of the officers in a very unfriendly voice. 'They're evidence.'

He dumps Anya's flying suit onto a desk and starts searching the pockets.

In about two seconds he finds her gun.

He stares at it, opens it, sees it's loaded, stares at it some more, then takes it over to show the other officer.

They both give me and Anya a long look.

'We were in the war,' I say. 'It's left over.'

I see what the other officer is doing. Sitting with my flying suit on his desk, holding Celeste's letter. Reading it. Or trying to.

'That's private,' I say.

'I think you mean secret,' says the officer.

He waves the letter at me.

'What is it?' he says. 'Instructions from Moscow?'

That sounds like one of those questions where the person already thinks they know the answer, so I don't bother replying.

The officer picks up one of Zelda's drawings.

He studies it closely.

'That's private too,' I say. 'It belongs to a war hero who was killed by the Nazis.'

The police officer frowns. He stands up and brings the scorched and crumpled piece of paper over to the cell.

'This diagram,' he says. 'What is it?'

'It's not a diagram,' I say. 'It's a drawing. A six-year-old girl did it to cheer herself up.'

'These chickens,' says the police officer. 'What do they mean?'

I sigh.

If this is what all the Australian police are like, I might as well just lie down in the street and wait for Zliv to cut me open.

'We've got important chicken farms in this region,' says the police officer. 'An alien invasion force would be looking for food supplies. So tell me, what do these chickens mean?'

'They mean,' I say to him, 'that Zelda liked chickens.'

The police officer gives me a scowl and goes back to his desk.

I give him a scowl in return.

When he and the other officer came to the clothes shop, I told them exactly who Anya and me are. They didn't even let me finish explaining about Ken and our tour of Australia. Just accused me of making up stupid stories.

Well even if I had been, my story wouldn't be as stupid as his one about chicken-farm invasions.

I feel Anya tugging my shirt.

'All I can think of,' she says quietly, 'is trying to get in touch with Ken and the others. In case any of them are still alive, to let them know where we are.'

'Good thought,' I say. 'But how?'

Anya reaches inside the folds of her new frock and pulls out the flare pistol, just for a second, then puts it back.

'You're amazing,' I whisper.

'Yeah, well calm down,' mutters Anya. 'I've only got one flare left. So we've only got one chance.'

She flicks her eyes towards the ceiling.

I see what she means. A small window, up high, with bars but no glass.

'We need to distract the officers,' she says.

'I'll do it,' I say.

I take my glasses off and put them safely under the bench. Then I go to the bars.

'Excuse me,' I say to the officers. 'I need to pee.'

'Bucket in the corner of the cell,' says one of the officers without looking up.

'I need some privacy,' I say. 'In my country that's how we always do it.'

'Plus,' says Anya loudly, 'the smell of male urine is dangerous for a pregnant woman. It can bring on a birth too early.'

I look at Anya. I've never heard that. It's probably not true, but what a great imagination.

One of the police officers gives a loud sigh, comes over, unlocks the cell bars, grabs the front of my shirt and marches me across the office.

'It's this way,' he says. 'I'll be with you the whole time, watching every drip.'

I use a trick a partisan showed me once. It's how you unbalance a person. But I change it slightly. Instead of cutting the ligaments behind the officer's knees with a knife, I use the edge of a chair, pulling it hard into the back of his legs.

As he topples, I pull myself free and hurl myself towards the office door.

I know it's locked, I saw them do it. But that's not the point. I just want their attention on me.

I get it.

I also get both their big heavy bodies, flattening me onto the floor.

Nearby there's a loud pop and a hiss.

The police officers roll off me. They stare into the cell.

Anya is standing on the bench, arms raised, pointing the barrel of the flare gun between the window bars.

Through the window we can see a small patch of sky, lit up by a red glow.

'Poop,' says one of the police officers. 'She's sent a signal. A code message in communist red.'

'That does it,' says the other officer, his voice wet and hot in my ear. 'You stupid mongrels are very much gunna wish you hadn't done that. I'm ringing Melbourne.'

Maybe Melbourne is where the good police are. The ones who'll listen. The ones who'll believe what we're telling them. Instead of leaving us here all night in a cold dark cell.

I roll over, trying to get comfortable on the stone floor. It's not easy. This blanket is very thin. I lived in an abandoned cellar in a wartime Polish ghetto once and the blankets weren't this thin.

Suddenly the cell light comes on.

Loud voices, close.

Squinting, I find my glasses.

Above me, on the wooden bench, Anya props herself up on an elbow, blinking.

'Alright, you two,' says one of the police officers. 'You've got visitors.'

The cell door swings open and two men come in. They're both wearing dark suits. They don't smile or say hello or do any of the friendly things visitors usually do.

I get up and stand between them and Anya.

'You might as well sit,' one of the men says to me. 'We'll be here for a while. And we won't be dancing.'

They're still not smiling.

'I'm Mr Petrie,' says the man. 'This is Mr Chase.'

I'm not saying hello if they're not.

I sit next to Anya. We look at the men without saying anything.

'So,' says Mr Chase. 'Quite an adventure you two have been having.'

'There's been a mistake,' I say. 'We're not Russian spies. Those police officers have been reading too many library books.'

Mr Chase does a little smile.

Just with his mouth.

'We know you're not spies,' he says. 'We know exactly who you are, and why you were brought to Australia. We know about Mr Ken Matthews' mission for the Australian government. Your roles in it. Or rather the role of one of you.'

I know you shouldn't interrupt men in suits, but I can't stop myself.

'Is Ken alright?' I say. 'And the others?'

Mr Chase thinks about this for a moment.

'We found the plane,' he says. 'The remains of five bodies were on board. I'm sorry.'

Anya and I swap a look.

I can see she's feeling as sad as I am.

Poor Simmo and the others. Including Ken, who didn't turn out to be a very nice person, but still.

I pull myself together.

Gabriek taught me how in wartime, whenever sad or shocking things happen, you mustn't forget about the mission.

'We can still do it,' I say to Mr Chase and Mr Petrie. 'We don't need the plane. We can still tell the Australian people what a great job their family members did in Europe. We can still bring sad and happy tears to their eyes.'

'That's a kind offer,' says Mr Chase. 'But the project has been terminated. Your services are no longer needed.'

I stare at him, horrified.

I know what terminated means.

Terminated means my photo won't be in the ncwspapcrs, not the Australian or the Polish ones. Terminated means now there'll be nothing to make Zliv believe my letter. Terminated means he'll try to track me down in Poland instead, and when he discovers I'm gone he'll take it out on Gabriek.

Who will still be in Poland, because terminated also means no places on a boat for him and Celeste.

'Please,' I say to the two men. 'We want to do the mission. Let us. Please.'

'Calm down,' says Mr Chase. 'You're not in any trouble. If you co-operate with us, you can stay in Australia. But before we go any further, I need you to answer some questions. Truthfully.'

He takes something from the inside pocket of his jacket.

A photograph of a man.

The man is looking over his shoulder, scowling. I don't think he liked having his photo taken.

'Do you know him?' says Mr Chase.

Anya and I study the photo. Anya shakes her head. I study it some more. The man is ugly and brutal-looking. He reminds me of somebody else. I'm starting to get a bad feeling.

'Recently,' says Mr Chase, 'this man approached the Australian consular officials in Poland. Making enquiries. About you, Felix.'

I shiver.

And not just because this cell is cold.

'I think I know who he is,' I say. 'I think I knew his brother.'

My head is spinning. That was quick. The postal service in Poland must be improving. Or maybe my letter was sent as a telegram. Sometimes, since the war, when postal deliveries are hopeless, kind postmasters send letters as telegrams.

'His name is Zlivandel Dragomir,' says Mr Chase. 'Gangster, mercenary, killer for hire. How do you know him, Felix? How do you know a man like this? And his brother?'

Mr Chase and Mr Petrie are both looking at me suspiciously.

'Isn't it obvious?' says Anya. 'Felix is planning a career as a professional gangster. He's studying to be a mercenary. Zliv used to help him with his hired-killer homework. Idiots.'

Mr Chase ignores Anya.

'I asked you a question, Felix,' he says.

I tell them about Gogol's death and Zliv blaming me. I tell them about my letter. Everything.

When I finish, Mr Chase and Mr Petrie don't say anything for a while. They look a bit stunned.

'The Australian officials in Poland,' says Anya. 'Did they arrest Zliv?'

Mr Chase shakes his head.

Anya swears in Polish under her breath.

'You don't have to worry,' says Mr Chase. 'Even if Dragomir makes it to Australia, which is very unlikely, he won't have any possible way of finding out where you'll be.'

'Where will we be?' I say.

'Living arrangements have been made for you,' says Mr Chase.

Living arrangements always make me nervous. The Nazis used to talk about them. When what they really meant was dying arrangements.

'What sort of living arrangements?' I say.

'A place has been found for each of you,' says Mr Chase. 'In children's homes.'

I struggle to take this in. I can't even speak.

'A boys' home for you,' says Mr Chase. 'A girls' home for you, young lady.'

'We thought that was better,' says Mr Petrie, still not smiling, 'than the other way around.'

'She's pregnant,' I yell at them. 'Anya can't have her baby in a children's home.'

'She'll be fine,' says Mr Chase. 'We've chosen a girls' home with very good facilities and a lot of experience in having babies adopted.'

Anya's scream is so sudden and so loud that for a moment I freeze.

So do Mr Chase and Mr Petrie.

Until they see that in Anya's hand is the half-full urine bucket, and she's swinging it at Mr Chase's head.

This car is like a Nazi car.

Big and black, with cruel and heartless people in the front. And completely innocent people in the back, handcuffed.

Me and Anya are doing what sensible people do in a Nazi car.

Staying silent. Not even a whisper. We don't want Mr Chase or Mr Petrie to have a single clue about what we're planning to do.

When they first made us get into this car, after Mr Chase had finished sponging his suit, I had the thought that me and Anya would be safe if we spoke in Polish.

But then, as we drove off into the night, I had another thought.

What if Mr Chase and Mr Petrie speak Polish?

That's very likely.

If I was the boss of the government secret-agent department, choosing agents to deal with us, I'd go for Polish-speaking ones.

So we haven't said a word.

For the first part of the journey Anya and I just kept looking at each other, making sure we both know what we're going to do.

Then Anya held my hand and put her head on my shoulder, and she's been asleep ever since.

Hours, driving through the night.

I'm listening to a sporting match playing quietly on the car radio. A sport called cricket, which I've never heard of.

The sporting match is being played in England. Which is much closer to Poland than Australia is, so it's making me feel a bit homesick.

And after tonight's conversation with Mr Chase and Mr Petrie, hearing that Zliv might be on his way, I'm also feeling a bit excited. And scared.

But not as homesick and scared as I would be without my precious things.

Zelda's drawing.

Celeste's letter.

Cyryl's gold ring.

My baby book.

Mr Chase made the police give them back. I'm hugging them to my chest in a big police envelope. They're helping me relax. So I can plan what I'm going to do after we drop Anya off and I get to where I'm going.

My very temporary home.

The car is slowing down. We're turning off the road into a long driveway.

'This is you, young lady,' says Mr Petrie.

I give Anya a gentle shake, then I peer out the window to see what sort of place they've brought her to. I'm hoping it's a place with nuns. I spent four years when I was little in an orphanage run by nuns. They were very strict, but mostly kind as well.

I want Anya to be as comfortable and happy as she can be while she's waiting for me to come back and help her get out of here.

Good. As far as I can see in the moonlight, this place looks a bit like the orphanage in Poland. It's an old stone building and some of the windows look religious.

And I think I can see a nun.

The car stops.

Mr Petrie gets out and opens Anya's door.

Anya is still holding my hand. We look at each other. Her face seems to be shining, even though the interior light of the car is quite dull.

Shining with all the friendship we've shared.

And all the love.

As we let go of each other's hands, I see Anya's expression change. I feel mine change too. We give each other a look that's not quite so soft and warm and friendly.

But very clear.

A fierce powerful promise that we'll be together again very soon.

Maybe my new home will be less scary than it looks at a distance. I mustn't panic too soon.

Dawn light always makes things look grey and shadowy.

Plus my eyes are very tired with all the effort of staying awake since we left Anya's place. Trying to remember all the roads and turnings so I can find my way back there.

These dark unfriendly buildings we're driving towards could actually be very religious and full of kind helpful nuns.

I hope they are.

No, they're not.

Our car is going through some very unfriendly looking gates and now I can see every detail of the ugly stained concrete buildings.

No religious windows.

High fences with barbed wire.

Not a nun in sight.

'This is you,' says Mr Petrie.

A man in short trousers and a short-sleeved shirt is waiting for us in front of a building.

He's as old as Gabriek, but a different shape. Sort of plump. And it's not just the man's trousers and sleeves that are short. The rest of him is too.

I hope he's nicer than he looks. I hope he's just frowning grumpily because it's so early.

Mr Petrie stops the car in front of the man.

Mr Chase gets out and opens my door.

'Don't be a smart alec with this bloke,' he says quietly. 'Not if you want to stay healthy.'

He stands back and I get out.

'Name,' says the man.

When he speaks, his cheeks jiggle. Although he's got an unfriendly voice, I stay calm. The first part of my plan is not to look like who I really am. A boy who'll be escaping from this place very soon.

'Felix Salinger,' I say.

'Go through that door,' says the man, pointing to a side doorway in the nearest building, 'and take all your clothes off.'

For a second I'm not sure I understood him properly.

I stare at him, probably not looking much like a boy who's going to be polite and obedient.

'On the double,' says the man.

I walk towards the building and go in through the doorway.

Into a small room.

So small, it's almost like a little storage room, with shelves on the walls and hooks under them.

I pause.

Where I come from, because it's often very cold, people don't take their clothes off unless there's a good reason.

I try to think of a reason.

It doesn't take me long.

This is a boys' home. All the boys here probably wear a uniform. That makes sense.

Except there isn't a uniform on any of the hooks.

Of course. I get it. This must be for hygiene. The people here probably haven't got a clue about my previous life. For all they know I could have very poor washing habits. So I bet the first thing they do with every new boy is make him have a bath.

I take my clothes off.

Outside I hear the car drive away.

The man comes into the room. He looks me up and down, which feels a bit strange because I'm completely naked.

'Follow me,' he says.

He walks out of the room, into the harsh early morning sunlight.

I follow.

This feels even more strange, walking along in the outside air with no clothes on.

The man goes up some steps and unlocks some big wooden double doors.

I follow him in.

The man locks the doors again and we walk down a gloomy corridor. There are rooms on either side, but I don't think anybody is in them. I'm glad, given that the only part of my body that's covered is the part behind my hands.

This corridor is quite long.

I don't get it. Why is the bath so far from the changing room?

More double doors. Also locked.

I'm starting to have an unpleasant feeling. One that's even more unpleasant than being naked. I'm starting to think this place might not be as easy to escape from as I'd hoped.

The man unlocks the second lot of doors and I follow him through.

And stop.

We're not in the corridor any more. We're in a large room full of long tables. Sitting at the tables are boys.

All staring at me.

Every muscle in my body wants to turn and run.

I manage not to.

No matter what's going to happen next, I still need to show I'm not a troublemaker.

I try to look relaxed and friendly.

I tell myself that in a room full of boys wearing shorts and shirts, it's always the one who's not that gets stared at.

'Stand on the table,' the man says to me.

I hesitate.

The man doesn't. He grabs me under the arms and lifts me up onto the nearest table.

'Hands on your head,' he says.

Now I've felt how strong he is, I obey.

I stand with my hands on my head. The boys look up at every part of me.

I'm not feeling even a tiny bit relaxed and friendly now.

'Boys,' says the man in a booming voice. 'This is Salinger. He'll be living with us from now on. As you know, I don't like secrets. A community thrives on honesty, which is why we have this little arrival ceremony. It reminds us that we have nothing to hide from each other. Remember that, boys, and please welcome Salinger.'

The boys all mutter 'Gerday'.

They don't look the slightest bit welcoming, not even the very young ones.

'Get down,' the man says to me.

I get down from the table.

Another man hands me shorts and a shirt, same as the other boys are wearing.

I put them on.

They're old and a bit ragged. I wonder what's happened to the clothes that Jack bought me, but I don't say anything.

The other man takes me to an empty space at a table. I sit down. A metal plate and cup are on the table in front of me. There's porridge on the plate and water in the cup.

None of the other boys look at me. They're all eating, so I do too.

The porridge has maggots in it.

Where I come from that's pretty normal so it doesn't bother me too much. I feel sorry for the other boys, though, if they're not used to it.

What a strange meal.

Nobody has spoken a word to me since I sat down. Or to each other.

When I went to live in the forest with the partisan fighters, they weren't very talkative either. But that was mostly because when we were above ground having meals, we had to keep quiet in case the Nazis were listening.

Maybe it's the same here. There's a table at the end of the room where the man who made the speech is eating with about six other men.

If a boy drops a spoon, or his porridge goes down the wrong way and he has a coughing fit, the men glare at him. When that happens, the boy looks scared. So do the boys around him.

I eat my porridge and maggots slowly and carefully. Before I've finished, the man who made the speech stands up and blows a whistle.

All the boys stand up as well, so I do.

The man signals to me to sit back down. The other boys all file silently out of the room. The man signals me to stand up again and to follow him.

He leads me down the corridor to one of the

other rooms, which is an office. We go in and he closes the door behind us.

'My name,' he says, 'is Mr Scully.'

I'm not sure if I should reply.

'Hello,' I say.

Mr Scully gives me an angry look.

'Sir,' he says.

'Sir,' I say. 'Sorry, sir.'

Mr Scully nods and his face slowly relaxes. Which makes me hope he's decided that I'm not the sort of troublemaker who'll be out of here in twenty-four hours, twelve if I can manage it.

Which is good.

'Salinger,' says Mr Scully. 'You'll find this is not a bad place to live, as long as you remember one thing. Here we practise fairness. For example, we all receive food and shelter here, so of course it's only fair that we should all work to provide that food and shelter.'

He nods towards the window.

Outside, I see, boys are digging up potatoes in a field. Beyond the field are other fields, with other boys doing things like ploughing and chopping and dragging rocks.

I see something else.

All the fields are inside a fence.

A long high fence with barbed wire on the top.

'Let me give you another example of what I mean by fairness,' says Mr Scully. 'The rules here benefit us all. If you break the rules, we all suffer.'

I nod to show I understand.

'Rule-breakers,' says Mr Scully, 'are punished. Does that seem fair to you?'

'Yes, sir,' I say.

'Pull your trousers down and bend over the desk,' says Mr Scully.

I look at him, confused.

'You haven't broken any rules,' says Mr Scully. 'But it's only fair that I show you exactly what will happen if you do. Bend over the desk.'

I can see a worn patch on the shiny top of the desk. Slowly I pull my shorts down. As I bend over and my tummy and private part press against the worn patch, I wish that the uniform here included underwear.

'I'm only going to do this once,' says Mr Scully. 'If I was actually punishing you, I would do it many times.'

Out of the corner of my eye, I see him pick up a strip of leather. At first I think it's a belt. But it seems to be springy, as if it's got metal in it. And hanging from the tip are other pieces of leather, thin and knotted.

Mr Scully raises the leather object over his head.

I close my eyes.

I remind myself I've been in war and been punched and stabbed and almost blown up several times and had very bad pain and survived.

Mr Scully grunts. I hear a loud swish.

Oh.

'You can stand up now,' says Mr Scully's voice from a long way away.

Before I do, I try to breathe.

Doctor Zajak always said that breathing is the most important part of dealing with pain this bad.

I take a breath, but it turns into a sob.

So does the next one.

'Stand up,' says Mr Scully, sounding annoyed.

I stand up, still sobbing more than breathing.

Not just because of the pain. Also because of something else.

Anya and I spent a lot of time in our gun turret in the clouds talking about how Australia would be full of good things.

We were wrong.

Maybe I'm wrong about this too.

It's only my first night here, so it's natural to make a few mistakes.

The mumbling and muttering I can hear in this dormitory might not be boys awake. It might just be them having nightmares. About how hard it is to get potatoes out of sunbaked soil. And how it's against the rules to complain. And what happens if you do.

Just thinking of Mr Scully's leather strap makes me shudder. Shuddering makes pain stab through my injured parts.

I'm not waiting any longer. I'm getting out of here. Sometimes you have to take a risk and I'm taking one that these boys are all asleep.

I slide out of bed, careful not to gasp noisily as I have more strap pain.

I put my glasses on. My envelope of precious things is already inside my shirt. No point looking for my shoes, I haven't seen them since I took them off in the changing room.

I'm ready for the journey back to Anya's place.

Ow.

Bare feet are quieter than shoes on a wooden floor, but in the moonlight you can't see splinters. I manage to muffle the yelp and creep past the other beds to the door.

This first part shouldn't be difficult.

I listened carefully when Mr Scully locked the dormitory door. I didn't hear him pull the key out. So it's still in the other side of the door.

Crouching down, I slide Zelda's drawing under the door so most of it is on the other side. Then I push a piece of thick fencing wire that I picked up in the potato field into the keyhole, probing until I feel the tip of it touching the end of the key. I push and dislodge the key, hoping it doesn't bounce off the paper on the other side and clatter away somewhere.

I hear the key hit the paper.

No clatter.

Slowly I drag the paper towards me. The gap under the door is just big enough for the key to come through.

'Thank you, Zelda,' I say silently. 'And Yuli.'

My partisan mother wasn't my real mother, but she taught me lots of important things. This has turned out to be one of the most useful.

I put Zelda's drawing back inside my shirt and

as quietly as I can I unlock the door. Outside I lock it again and leave the key in the keyhole.

Here's hoping I can do the same with the main door of the dormitory building.

I creep along the passage, reach the main door, crouch down at the keyhole and peer into it.

Moonlight. The keyhole is empty.

I stand up and try to think fast. Maybe there's a window somewhere that's not locked.

All the ones in the dormitory are. But I heard one of the boys say that the men in charge here all have bedrooms at the other end of the building. If I can find a heavy sleeper who likes a bit of fresh air through his open window . . .

As I turn towards the other end of the building, I thank Yuli for also teaching me how to go into a room silently.

A large figure blocks my way.

'Where do you think you're going?' hisses an indignant voice, and two big hands clamp around my neck.

In the gloom I can't see who it is.

Not Mr Scully. This person is too tall.

Then more moonlight comes in through the skylight over the door.

It's a boy. I noticed him today in the potato field because of his size. He doesn't look much older than me, just taller, wider and thicker.

Big head, big arms and big hands.

'Let go,' I wheeze. 'Or I'll hurt you.'

'Oh, yeah?' hisses the boy. 'How are you going to do that?'

I decide to tell him rather than show him.

'I had a partisan mother once,' I say. 'She could kill with her bare hands. There's a place on your throat, I can see it now. If I jab it hard, I'll send a blood clot so deep into your brain you won't know what day it is. Somebody else will have to carve the date on your gravestone.'

Gabriek taught me how when you're threatening somebody, doing it with a bit of humour makes it even scarier.

The boy looks uncertain. His big hands loosen around my throat, then go tight again.

'That's bull,' he says.

'Listen to my accent,' I say. 'Where would you say I'm from? An Australian church choir or a forest hideout full of ruthless partisans and killers in Nazi-occupied Poland?'

The boy's hands stay where they are.

'You don't scare me,' he says, his voice wobbling a bit. 'There are rules here and you've broken one.'

I don't know why this boy is so worried about rules, and suddenly I don't care. His hands are too tight around my throat. I lose my temper.

'Listen to me,' I hiss. 'I've travelled thousands of miles to get away from war. But if I have to, I'll fight one here. Back off in the next five seconds or I'll kill you.'

I start counting.

The boy lets go of my neck and takes a step back.

We stare at each other, both trembling. The boy because he thinks I meant it, and me because up till the count of four I did.

Suddenly, the boy sags.

My throat still hurts, but there's something about his big round droopy shoulders that makes me feel sorry for him. If he's in this place, chances are his parents are dead.

Before I can let him know we've got something in common, he sticks his face close to mine again.

'Just don't forget the rule,' he says, trying to sound tough again. 'The rule is I'm the only one who does the thing with the paper and the key. So if you want to sneak down to the kitchen and steal food, you get permission from me and then you share the food with me.'

'I don't want to steal food,' I say. 'So get lost.'

I turn away from him.

Too quickly. My envelope of precious things slips out of my shirt and thuds to the floor.

The baby book slides towards the boy's feet.

He picks it up and looks at it.

'I get the picture,' he says. 'It's not food you steal, it's dirty books.'

I grab the book back from him.

The boy starts to say something else, but before he can, another voice rings out, an angry one.

'Gosling, what are you doing?'

I look round.

One of the men from Mr Scully's table in the dining room is coming towards us.

I grab my things and put them inside my shirt.

'I haven't seen today's roster,' growls the man, 'but I'm guessing, Gosling, that as you're up so early, you must be today's pig boy. Did Mr Olaf tell you to wait here? Or are you just lounging around wasting time?'

Before the boy can answer, the man turns to me.

'And you, new boy, if this lump of lard's showing you the ropes, you're not gunna learn how to be a pig boy standing here, are you? Shift your lazy carcasses, both of you.'

I can see the alarm on Gosling's face. I can see he wants to explain something to the man, probably about pigs. But I can see he doesn't dare.

The man unlocks the door and we follow him outside.

I understand why we're called pig boys now.

There's a pig.

'Oh, Jesus,' whimpers Gosling.

He's been carrying on like this ever since the man led us into this small hut, brought a pig in, and then left, locking the door.

In the dawn light I can see a knife hanging on the inside of the door. And a blood-stained apron. And hanging from the rafters are lots of hooks, big metal ones.

Empty hooks.

The floor, which is concrete, has grooves in it leading to a metal grille, so liquid can drain away.

I know what this place is.

I saw one like it when we did a partisan raid on the farm of a Nazi-sympathiser.

It's a slaughterhouse.

'I can't do it,' Gosling is whimpering. 'I can't kill an innocent animal.'

I look at him, wondering how he's avoided doing it up till now. There's a roster, so all the boys must take turns. And with this many hungry boys, a lot of pigs must get killed.

'Haven't they made you do this before?' I say.

Gosling shakes his head.

'We've got a special deal,' he says. 'Mr Olaf and me. I go to his room some nights and he makes sure I'm never on the roster.'

I stare at Gosling, sympathetic.

But also horrified.

'It's not what you think,' mutters Gosling. 'I take him food and I'm teaching him chess.'

I sigh.

So far I don't like Gosling much, but one thing you learn in wartime, you don't blame a person for trying to survive.

Plus I know how he feels about killing innocent animals. I used to feel the same. But it all changes the first time you're so hungry your guts feel like they're eating themselves. Then, if somebody gives you a lump of pork fat, just one bite makes you understand why sometimes bad things have to be done for good reasons.

I put the apron on and take the knife off the door. Gosling whimpers again and turns his back to the pig and closes his eyes and puts his fingers in his ears.

I test the knife on a piece of straw.

It's very sharp, which is good.

I crouch next to the pig and whisper to it. About how I'm sorry our first meeting has to be like this. How I've been trained medically, so I know about cardiovascular systems. How I can promise it won't feel any pain.

Gently I put my hand over the pig's eyes.

I remember what Yuli told me about the Nazis she used to creep up on when they were doing bad things.

She said her job was to kill them, and if she was quick and quiet and her knife was sharp and she knew exactly where in their throats it should go, there was no need to make them suffer.

I take a deep breath, grip the knife hard, put my arm round the pig, and try my best to do what Yuli did.

Afterwards, when the meat is hanging up and the guts are in the buckets and I'm rinsing my hands and the knife, Gosling comes over.

'Thank you,' he says.

I don't reply.

I'm trying hard to think about all the hungry people who'll be grateful to the pig for giving up its life. The thought isn't making me feel any better, not as much as I hoped it would.

It's not the blood, I'm used to that. OK, there was more here than in a clean and heat, but blood is blood.

It's something else.

An experience I've never had before.

Taking a life instead of trying to save one.

Gosling shuffles his feet for a while and then clears his throat.

'Earlier,' he says, 'when you were sneaking out of the dorm, you were trying to escape, weren't you?'

I still don't reply.

I've just done him a big favour. The least he can do is see that I don't really feel like chatting.

'You can't escape from here,' says Gosling. 'Not from inside the fence. Scully used to run a military prison camp. The whole fence has got electrical alarms.'

I watch the last of the blood running down the drain and I think about how Anya is going to feel when they take her baby away from her.

I won't let that happen.

Somehow I won't.

'Nobody's ever escaped from inside the fence,' says Gosling.

When will he be quiet?

For a kid who's so concerned about innocent

creatures losing their lives, he's taking a very big risk, making me feel this annoyed while I've got a sharp knife in my hand.

Not really.

I put the knife down.

'I've been thinking a lot about it,' says Gosling. 'And I reckon there is a way to escape. Not over the fence. Another way.'

He's got my attention now.

I look at him.

His eyes are bright and it's hard to believe that five minutes ago he was a blubbering mess.

'What way?' I say.

'Cricket,' he says.

Maybe this is why the plumbing here is so bad and the beds are so uncomfortable and the food is so weevily and the educational activities are almost totally non-existent.

It's because Mr Scully spends most of the boys'-home money on cricket.

That would explain why these cricket nets next to the pig shed are so big and well-maintained and completely covered in very good netting.

'Bowl again,' yells Gosling.

He hunches over, tapping the dirt in front of the wicket with his bat.

I run up and bowl.

Gosling swings.

I know it's good netting because when Gosling hits the ball, he does it so hard you'd think the ball would rip through the net.

But it doesn't, and only very expensive tank-trap-quality netting is that strong.

This time, Gosling swings and misses.

The ball smashes into his stumps.

'Amazing,' yells Gosling.

He hurries towards me along the bowling strip, panting and beaming.

'Who'd have guessed,' he says. 'A kid from Poland, a demon bowler.'

He says that a lot, even though I've explained that if he'd seen the partisans training me to throw grenades, he wouldn't be surprised at all.

It's basically the same arm movement. Same balance. Same position of the feet. All I've done is speed it up and add a bit of spin.

'I reckon you're nearly ready,' says Gosling. 'Bit more batting practice and we'll show Scully what you can do. When he sees you bowl, I reckon you'll be in the team for the next match.'

We look at each other.

We know what that means.

I glance around to see if anyone else can hear us.

The other boys are working in the fields and the men are supervising them. Me and Gosling are on special privileges. When Gosling told Mr Scully he was training a new star for the cricket team, Mr Scully said we could have an hour in the nets every afternoon.

'Have you decided if you're coming with me?' I say to Gosling.

He looks at his bat. Rubs at a red mark.

'Of course,' he says. 'I'll be playing in the match.'

'You know what I mean,' I say.

Gosling steps closer to me. Puts the bat in my hands and makes it look like he's helping me with my batting posture.

'When my mum brought me here years ago,' he says quietly, 'she didn't want to. But she had to because she was very sick. She made me promise on the Bible not to run away. Then she didn't get better and I never saw her again. But I've kept the promise I made to her.'

I stare at him. That's crazy.

But I don't say anything.

You don't when somebody's mother is dead.

I could do it now.

Jump off this cricket bus as it slows down at the next dusty corner. Sprint across that field of corn. Keep sprinting till I get to the girls' home.

No, too risky.

I would have jumped when I was younger. And more hopeful. And convinced that things mostly turn out good.

But one of the bad things about being fourteen is you know how the world works. You've learned how easily things can go wrong.

The only way off this bus while we're moving is through this window. It'd be a tight squeeze, so I couldn't be certain about landing on my feet. And it's very hard to make a quick clean getaway after you've landed on your head.

'Nearly there,' says Gosling.

I know what he's saying.

Better to stick to the original plan. Make my escape from the cricket pitch.

Rescue Anya that way.

'Thanks,' I say to him.

I'm very grateful to Gosling. He's very generous, teaching me about cricket. Helping me get into the team. Sharing his escape plan even though he won't benefit from it.

So I don't mind sitting next to him.

Despite the smell.

The problem is that the boys' home doesn't have much hot water. The rest of us manage to wash in cold water when we have to, but Gosling can't do that. He says his mum got sick from washing in cold water.

'Look out,' he suddenly whispers. 'Scully.'

I'm glad I'm not halfway out the bus window. Mr Scully is coming towards us from his seat at the front. He's looking right at me.

'So, Salinger,' he says. 'Big day for you.'

'Yes, sir,' I say. 'It is.'

I don't tell him why in particular.

'Your first match for us,' says Mr Scully. 'You must be excited. And what a match. Thirteen times we've played the Taranga town team and thirteen times we've lost. But I have a feeling that's all going to change today. We're counting on you, Salinger.'

Mr Scully shakes my hand.

Behind me, a couple of boys gasp.

Mr Scully is moving his mouth in a strange way. I think he's smiling.

'Thank you, sir,' I say.

Mr Scully heads back to his seat.

Gosling gives me a stern look.

'Just don't forget,' he whispers. 'Make sure you take some wickets today before you do a runner.'

Cricket has made me good at maths.

I've taken five wickets today for a total of sixty-three runs. That's an average of twelve-point-six runs a wicket.

Mr Scully is looking very happy about that.

Gosling is good at maths too. Which is why he encouraged me to develop my long-distance ball-throwing skills. So I got chosen to field out here on the boundary.

This way, as soon as the ball is clobbered over to the other side of the pitch and everyone's attention is over there, I can dash into the trees. With, Gosling calculated, a fifty percent bigger start on all the adults in the pavilion than if I was fielding in the slips.

I shouldn't have to wait too long.

The Taranga batsmen are licking their lips. The boy bowling for us at the moment isn't very good. You can tell he's never had a grenade in his hand.

Shame. If I wasn't leaving, I could help him with his arm movement.

No, it's not a shame.

Time is running out for Anya.

By my calculations she's got about two weeks left till the baby comes. I need to get a move on.

The loud whack of leather on wood jolts me out of my baby maths.

Yes. That's the sort of big hit that'll get people's attention over to the opposite boundary.

Except I can't see the ball.

It must be high in the air.

Poop. It's in the air all right. Heading in the wrong direction. Coming towards me.

'Catch!' everyone in our team starts screaming.

I run backwards to get myself under it. I think about changing the plan. Dropping the catch and making sure the ball bounces over the boundary and into the trees. Chasing it and disappearing into the trees myself at high speed.

Sure, everyone would be watching, but I'd be out of sight with a big start.

Then I see Gosling sprinting from further along the boundary. I can see from his face how much he wants to catch the ball.

In his future life in that horrible boys' home, a catch like this would help him a lot.

Except he's not going to get here in time, poor bloke.

Suddenly I know what I'm going to do. A small gift to say thank you for all of Gosling's generous help and friendship.

It means I'll have to stay a bit longer, but I can bowl another over and make my escape after that.

The ball is plummeting towards me out of the sun. I dive backwards as if I'm making a last moment adjustment to get under the ball. It smacks into my hands at the same time as my back thuds against the ground. I pretend the impact has jolted the ball out of my hands. I flick the ball back up into the air.

Gosling is three paces away.

He takes two and dives.

And wraps his big hands round the ball.

Our team erupts. As I pick myself up, I can see Mr Scully and his colleagues over in the pavilion throwing their hats into the air.

All our team are racing across the pitch towards me and Gosling, screaming and yelling.

It was a good catch, but why are they so excited? There's more to be done to win this match.

Then I see something that sends a chill through my digestive tract.

Both Taranga batsmen are leaving the pitch.

I must have got the maths wrong. That must have been their last wicket. They must be all out. The match must be over. We must have won.

Oh no.

Standing here doing the baby maths, I didn't pay enough attention to the cricket maths.

I feel sick.

I've wasted my chance to get away.

The next match might not be for weeks.

Ecstatic team members are crowding around, hugging me and Gosling. If they weren't holding me up, I'd be slumping miserably down onto the grass.

'Stand on the table,' says Mr Scully.

I don't want to, but I don't argue. At least this time I'm fully clothed.

I climb up onto one of the tables in the dining room. Gosling climbs up next to me.

All around us, boys clap and cheer and stamp their feet.

I sigh. The match was three days ago. You'd think all the fuss would have died down by now.

But no. Mr Scully just announced after dinner that he has something special to show us from our famous victory. So here we are, up on the table. At least Gosling looks like he's enjoying it.

'All hail,' says Mr Scully, 'to our heroes.'

I sigh again.

It was just a cricket match. If you've ever met a real hero, someone for example who sacrifices their life to try and protect children, you'll know that it's extremely unlikely for a cricket match to produce one hero, let alone two.

Mr Scully picks up a newspaper.

It's just a local paper, but from the way he spreads it out and holds it up so all the boys can see it, he obviously feels it's more important than *The New York Times*.

MIRACLE CATCH ENDS DROUGHT
FOR BOYS' HOME

That's what the headline says on the page he's showing them. And there's a smaller headline.

FROM WAR WAIF TO AUSSIE HERO

Underneath is a photo of me and Gosling.

I've got a strange expression on my face in the photo. Seeing it now, I know why. I can remember exactly what I was thinking on Saturday while it was being taken.

I was thinking about Anya. About how much time is ticking away. I was wondering if the nuns are getting ready to take her baby.

I was also wondering if copies of *The Taranga Bugle* ever turn up in Polish libraries.

The boys didn't notice my tense expression on Saturday and they haven't noticed it now in the photo. They're just cheering and stamping.

I've never seen Mr Scully look so happy.

'Come in, boys,' says Mr Scully.

Now that we're in his office, he doesn't look as happy as he just did in the dining room.

'Right,' he says. 'We've had our celebration, now I want to talk to you about something else.'

He's not looking happy at all.

He can't blame us that it took fourteen years to beat the Taranga town team. That would be crazy.

'Salinger,' says Mr Scully. 'I was watching you on Saturday when you were fielding on the boundary.'

Gosling, standing next to me, shuffles his feet.

I wish he wouldn't.

Feet that size can give things away.

'I was puzzled,' says Mr Scully. 'Something about the way you were standing. Something about the way you were watching the batsmen. A little movement you made every time a batsman hit the ball hard.'

'I taught him that, sir,' says Gosling in a wobbly voice. 'I taught him a good fielder is always alert.'

'Be quiet,' says Mr Scully.

Gosling swallows noisily.

'Since Saturday afternoon,' says Mr Scully, 'I've been thinking about it a lot. And this morning I realised what was going on. You weren't being an alert fielder, Salinger. Not for our benefit, anyway. You were planning to escape.'

I try to look shocked.

'No, sir,' I say.

I wish Mr Scully was staring hard at Gosling instead of at me. Gosling is looking genuinely shocked. And terrified.

Mr Scully picks up his springy leather strap.

Gosling gives a little whimper.

'I know it was just you,' says Mr Scully to me. 'Gosling doesn't have the intelligence or the bravery to plan an escape. Whereas you, Salinger, with your exotic background, you're perfectly capable.'

I don't say anything.

There's no point.

Mr Scully is right, and he knows he is.

'So I've brought you both in here to explain something to you,' says Mr Scully.

He starts slapping the strap onto the palm of his hand. Hard.

I swallow.

The last time Mr Scully brought me in here to explain something, I was in pain for days.

'If,' says Mr Scully, looking at me with an icy expression, 'and it's a big if, but if at any point you do manage to escape, I will flog your friend. I will flog Gosling each day you are absent. Fifty times.'

Gosling whimpers louder than he did when he was pig boy.

'Each and every day,' says Mr Scully. 'Do you understand?'

'Yes, sir,' I say.

I do understand, completely.

I understand that when I escape, which needs to be very soon, I'll have to take Gosling with me.

Maybe you can help me, Richmal Crompton.
Please.

Show me a way to get out of here.

One that doesn't involve triggering the fence alarm or waiting weeks for the next cricket match. One that gets me to Anya in time for the baby.

Anything, Richmal Crompton, please.

'Salinger,' hisses Gosling in my ear. 'Wake up.'

I sit up, blinking, and fumble around for my glasses, careful not to knock my cricket bat over.

The dormitory is dark. I can only just make out the shape of Gosling next to my bed.

'What is it?' I whisper.

'There's a bloke outside who wants to see you,' says Gosling.

I stare at him.

My heart starts to hammer.

It's the middle of the night. Australians are friendly, but not that friendly.

I do some frantic maths. I try to work out how many days since I left Poland. Whether it's enough time for a revenge-crazed killer to bribe his way onto a plane to Australia.

Lots of days.

Plenty of time.

'This man,' I say to Gosling. 'Does he have an accent like mine?'

Gosling looks uncertain.

'Not sure,' he says. 'Quiet spoken sort of bloke. I don't think so. He might have.'

I grab my cricket bat and hurry out past Gosling and his sheet of paper, which is still under the open dorm door.

There's no point in not going.

If it is Zliv, he'll find me anyway.

Better to meet him outside, away from the other boys. If he couldn't recognise me in the dark dorm, he might kill everyone just to be sure.

I stop and stare.

The main door of the dormitory building is wide open. I don't understand. Are there supervisors up and about?

Gosling is right behind me.

'I've got a key,' he says. 'I carved it out of very hard wood. It took me seven weeks.'

I stare at him.

'I like to go outside some nights,' he says. 'I don't mind living in this place as long as I can look at the stars.'

I'm starting to realise there's more to Gosling than I thought.

Quickly I tell him about Zliv.

Just the basics. Zliv's killing career. And why he wants me to be part of it.

I say I'll understand if Gosling would rather go back to the dorm and hide under the bedcovers.

Gosling's eyes have gone big.

But he doesn't move.

I pull him away from the door and make him stay behind me. This is my fight. Gosling can back me up if he wants to.

Gripping the cricket bat hard, I step warily out into the night.

I peer around.

I can't see anybody. I can hardly see anything.

Yes I can.

The moon has come out from behind a cloud. Across the quadrangle where Mr Scully counts us first thing each morning, I can see that a hole has been cut in the perimeter fence.

Which shouldn't be possible.

Gosling said the fence is wired with electrical alarms. Why aren't the sirens wailing? Why aren't the lights flashing?

I hurry over to the fence, looking anxiously around. I reach up and grab one of the sirens. It comes away easily in my hand. Just an empty tin cone with no wires attached.

Mr Scully must have lied about the alarms.

He must have installed fake security equipment to save money so he could build extra cricket nets.

Has Gosling just discovered this and decided he's kept the promise to his mother long enough?

Did he cut the fence so we could both escape?

It's possible. But what about the man who wants to see me?

Over my shoulder, Gosling gives a squeak.

Before I can turn round, somebody grabs me.

'Stay quiet,' whispers a voice into my ear.

Fear jolts through me. I struggle to get free. And unexpectedly, I do.

The voice whispers again.

'Sorry to startle you.'

I realise the voice is speaking English. No Polish accent. I turn round.

It's a man I've never seen before.

'Are you Felix Salinger?' says the man.

I nod. No point pretending. If he turns out to be Zliv in disguise I've got a cricket bat. The moon is still out and I can see the place under his chin that Yuli taught me about.

'You've taken some finding,' says the man. He smiles. 'Thank God for cricket.'

I'm starting to feel weak with relief.

'The name's Neal Fishbone,' says the man. 'I'm a journalist with a Melbourne newspaper. Chasing something the government seems to want to keep secret. An RAAF plane that came back to Australia with two young war survivors on board.'

I look at the man.

He's got an honest face.

That doesn't always mean anything, but this time I decide it's all I've got.

Plus he's from Melbourne, which is where I want to go with Anya.

'The plane crashed,' I say.

'I know,' says the journalist. 'Well, I suspected. After the end of the war there were claims some of our planes in Europe weren't being looked after too well. Spare parts being sold on the black market, stuff like that. Could be why the authorities want to keep this plane crash a secret.'

I take all this in.

'My paper wants to publish the details of you coming here,' says the journalist. 'You can go on the record if you like, or be a background source, which means we'll print the details but we won't say we spoke with you.'

I'm not sure what all that means.

One thing I am sure of, and I tell the journalist.

'The other young war survivor isn't here,' I say. 'We'll only tell you about our journey if we can do it together. Which means we have to go to where she is.'

The journalist thinks about this. I can see he's not totally enthusiastic, but tempted.

In the moonlight I spot something under the trees on the other side of the fence.

A car. It must be his.

'We should leave now,' I say to him.

While he thinks some more, I turn to Gosling.

'You have to come too,' I say.

Gosling looks panicked. I know he's thinking about the promise he made to his mother.

'Your mum,' I say to him. 'Sorry to ask, but was she married?'

Gosling hesitates, then shakes his head.

'So she was completely on her own,' I say. 'Looking after you and protecting you without any help.'

Gosling looks very sad at the thought. He nods.

'Same with my friend,' I say. 'And she needs our help, urgently.'

Gosling doesn't say anything.

Just starts biting his lip.

'I think your mother would understand,' I say. 'I think she wouldn't mind about you breaking your promise. Not if it's to help someone who's dealing with what she had to deal with.'

Gosling chews his lip some more.

Then he grabs my cricket bat.

'Let's go,' he says.

We get to the girls' home just after dawn. Less time than I thought it would take, but I know why.

When Mr Chase and Mr Petrie were driving me from here to the boys' home, I was so anxious about remembering every road and every turn, the journey seemed to take forever.

I'm glad I went to the trouble.

The map I made during my first night in the dorm has brought us straight here.

I tuck the map back into my envelope.

'He's extremely well organised,' says Gosling.

'I noticed,' says Neal.

Journalists probably like the world to be well organised.

Neal gives Gosling a look.

He's done it several times during the trip.

I think it's because of the smell. He's probably starting to worry now that we've pulled up outside the main gate of the girls' home. He's probably wondering how the nuns are going to cope when they meet Gosling.

He doesn't have to worry.

We won't be hanging around.

'I'll go and see the folks here,' says Neal. 'Find out if they can give us somewhere private for our talk with Anya.'

'No,' I say. 'We can't talk here. Anya has to leave straight away. We'll only talk after you've taken us somewhere else.'

Neal doesn't look happy. Has he forgotten what I explained to him an hour ago? All the things Anya is up against. How the nuns will take her baby.

Neal stayed silent when I told him, which at the time I thought was just him being shocked and horrified. Now I've got an awful feeling it was him having cold feet.

'Come on,' says Neal. 'That wasn't the deal.'

'We didn't have a deal about this part of it,' I say. 'I just said that me and Anya would talk to you together. Which we will do, in the car, driving away from here.'

'He's extremely stubborn too,' says Gosling.

Gosling's right.

I am being stubborn. And bossy. But sometimes in life, when you're arguing with a Nazi or dealing with a headstrong Polish chicken or trying to save your friend's baby, you have to be.

'Maybe it's best if you boys stay in the car,' says Neal. 'I'll try to find out where Anya is.'

I shake my head.

'Anya doesn't know you,' I say. 'She can be a bit prickly with men she doesn't know.'

Neal sighs.

'Alright,' he says. 'We'll all go.'

'Maybe it's best,' says Gosling, 'if a journalist isn't caught sneaking around in a girls' home. Specially with two young blokes he's just helped escape from a boys' home.'

Neal gives him a look.

'You could end up in the papers,' says Gosling.

Neal doesn't think that's funny. But after he gives it more thought, he says he'll stay in the car.

'I thought that was very funny,' says Gosling.

We're heading down a track that curves around towards the back of the girls' home.

It's still very early. I can't see anyone moving around near any of the buildings. But we keep our heads down just in case.

'A reporter,' chuckles Gosling. 'In the papers.'

'Shhh,' I say.

I just heard something.

A clanking sound.

I'm not sure what it is and I learned from the partisans to be extremely wary of any sound you can't identify.

'Keep your head down,' I whisper to Gosling.

I drag him behind a bush. We crouch and listen. The clanking gets louder.

'I know that sound,' says Gosling.

We peek out.

Two girls with sticks are herding cows along the track towards us. A couple of the cows have got big bells round their necks.

'Don't be scared,' says Gosling to me. 'Cows are just like pigs, only bigger.'

I ignore him.

We need information. So let's hope these girls won't scare easily and raise the alarm.

'Excuse me,' I say to the girls. 'Are you from the home?'

The girls look startled, which is understandable when two boys suddenly step out from behind a bush.

'If we are,' says one of the girls, trying to sound tough, 'what's it to you?'

'We're looking for our friend,' I say. 'She's in the home too. Anya Goszinka.'

Both the girls stop trying to be tough and start looking sad instead.

'Poor Anya,' says one.

'I really feel for her,' says the other.

'Why?' I say. 'What's happened?'

'Come and see for yourself,' says the first girl.

The girls hide me and Gosling in among the cows. They steer us all together through a gate and into a large milking shed.

The cows don't seem to mind us being with them. I don't either. It feels safe here, surrounded by huge slow-moving bodies and warm breath. Until a dog barks nearby and the cows get nervous and we're almost knocked off our feet.

'Watch out for the horns,' mutters Gosling. 'The front end of a cow is different to a pig.'

The girls quieten the cows down. They take me and Gosling through a door at the end of the shed and into the main building of the girls' home.

Everyone is at breakfast, nuns included.

With the girls guiding us, we creep past the dining hall and up some stairs.

One of the girls points down a corridor.

'Anya's in the dorm at the end,' she says. 'We're off to breakfast or we'll be missed. Be careful, and if the nuns get you, leave us out of it.'

I nod.

'Thanks,' I say.

I creep along the corridor, Gosling close behind. There are dormitories on both sides, all empty.

Except one.

A voice is coming from the end dorm.

I signal to Gosling to be quiet. I try not to make a sound myself as I peep round the doorway.

Anya is in a bed near the door, one arm across her tummy.

A nun is standing next to the bed.

'Is she there?' hisses Gosling behind me.

'Shhh,' I whisper. 'She's got company.'

I steer Gosling into an empty room next door. It's a small office, with a window that looks out over the beds, including Anya's.

I pull Gosling down out of sight.

The office window is open slightly and the nun's voice drifts in.

'You poor child,' she's saying. 'Such a burden for one so young. But it won't be much longer and then others will shoulder the burden for you. Eat your breakfast, pet, and I'll come and collect the tray when you've finished.'

I peek through the window.

The nun is putting a tray onto Anya's bed.

'Good breakfast,' mutters Gosling.

He's right. On the tray is a breakfast almost as delicious-looking as the one I had at the air base.

'Take your time, pet,' says the nun to Anya. 'Ring the bell when you're ready.'

What a nice nun.

At least Anya's well cared for here.

But Anya doesn't look happy. She's scowling. I'm guessing that's because of what the nun said about others shouldering her burden.

Meaning her baby.

The nun turns to leave.

Gosling and I duck down again. We wait till the nun's footsteps have faded away along the corridor, then hurry into Anya's dormitory.

Anya is slumped in bed, not even looking at the breakfast.

She sees us. She sits up, eyes wide with delight.

The tray almost slides onto the floor. She grabs it with one hand, grinning at us.

'Took your time,' she says.

I go over and give her a hug. The longest hug we've ever had. Both my arms round her, one of hers round me.

'There's a car waiting for us outside,' I say. 'And a friendly reporter. Let's go.'

Anya gives me a look. She pulls back the bed-clothes. Her other wrist is handcuffed to the metal bed frame.

Me and Gosling stare, shocked.

'Mean mongrels,' says Gosling.

'I tried to escape,' says Anya. 'Didn't get far in the heat. A blacksmith gave me a lift. Brought me straight back here. I think he supplies the nuns with their prison equipment.'

Anya yanks angrily at the handcuffs.

I feel the same as her, but we have to stay calm.

'Have you got a hairpin?' I say.

'Hairpins aren't allowed in this dump,' says Anya. 'Only visitors can have them and I haven't had visitors until now.'

She looks Gosling up and down.

'Pity you're not a girl,' she says.

'I've got a toothpick,' says Gosling. 'I carved it out of very hard wood.'

He hands me a small black toothpick.

It feels pretty hard. I kneel down and slip it into the keyhole of the handcuffs. I did this quite a lot when I used to repair locks with Gabriek in the city. Just not with a toothpick.

'This is Gosling,' I say to Anya, while I jiggle his toothpick.

Anya looks at him for a long moment.

'Thank you, Gosling,' she says. 'I'm glad you're not a girl.'

'Tyrone,' says Gosling. 'Tyrone Gosling.'

As the handcuffs click open, I stare at him.

Tyrone?

We creep out the way we came in, through the milking shed at the back of the girls' home.

As soon as we step into the shed, I see there's a problem.

A dog is in among the cows. Not a cattle dog. A local stray, by the look of it, crazed with hunger.

The cows are about to stampede. They're milling towards us with wild eyes.

'Get to the car,' says Gosling. 'I'll look after this.'

I hesitate, but he's right.

For a start, Anya doesn't know where the car is. And having to run with a tummy the size of hers, she needs somebody with her.

Gosling walks slowly towards the cows.

He growls softly, his big hands splayed in the air like a giant starfish.

The cows back away. Sort of.

Anya and I slip past Gosling and the cows. We hurry through the door at the other end of the shed. Behind us we hear barking and grunting and the thud of hooves.

I grab Anya's hand.

Just as well. A couple of times on the way to the car she looks over her shoulder, which makes her stumble.

I open the car door, but Anya hesitates.

'Hello,' says Neal from the driver's seat. 'You must be Anya. Probably best if you get in.'

I can see Anya wants to go back for Gosling. In her condition, she shouldn't even be thinking about something that risky.

'I'll go back,' I say.

But Anya gives a whoop.

'There he is.'

We scramble into the back of the car as Gosling sprints towards us.

Gosling throws himself into the front seat and even before he gets the door shut, Neal has the car sliding and rattling down the road.

'Are you OK?' I say to Gosling.

He doesn't seem to have any serious injuries. Just a few scratches and scrapes on his hands and face. No dog bites that I can see.

'I'm fine,' says Gosling.

He grins at me.

'Sorry,' he says. 'Should have brought back a few steaks.'

Anya leans forward in her seat and puts her hand on Gosling's shoulder.

'Thank you, Tyrone,' she says.

I'm feeling a bit dizzy. I don't know if it's all the stress, or Gosling's name.

'That poor old dog,' says Gosling. 'Didn't look like it had seen food for days. Lucky I had a bit of old sandwich in my pocket.'

Anya leaves her hand on Gosling's shoulder. She's gazing at him with an emotional expression.

Very emotional.

OK he deserves it. But still.

'Settle back, everyone,' says Neal. 'Hang on tight. Melbourne here we come.'

'**Maybe** we don't have to worry,' I say. 'Maybe the nuns won't call the police.'

We're driving fast along a rough dusty back road. It's so we can keep out of sight. But I wish we were on a main road. All this bumping isn't good for Anya's tummy.

'They probably won't call the police just yet,' says Neal. 'They'll probably want to keep the whole thing quiet till they've worked out how to explain it. But we can't be too careful.'

I look at Anya. She's very pale.

'I'm fine,' she says, touching my arm.

She pats her tummy.

'We both are.'

Anya and I start answering Neal's questions about our journey from Poland.

Gosling is sitting in the front next to Neal, and sometimes he has to hold the steering wheel so Neal can scribble things on his notepad.

A few times I see him looking at Anya in the rear-view mirror.

Neal, that is.

Well, Gosling too.

'No offence, Anya,' says Neal, 'but now I've met you, I'm not surprised the government wants to bury this whole thing. A girl of your age, about to give birth, flying in a military aircraft. It's a major scandal.'

'To be fair,' says Anya, 'I did stow away.'

Neal gives a laugh that's more like a snort.

'So much for military security,' he says. 'Doesn't fill a nation with confidence when a sixteen-year-old girl can waltz onto an RAAF bomber with the dried beef.'

I don't think that's totally fair towards military security. What Neal's saying is true of most sixteen-year-old girls, but he doesn't know Anya.

'Neal,' I say. 'For your article, why don't you let Anya tell you a bit more about herself. She's had a few experiences that the sixteen-year-olds you know might not have had.'

'Good idea,' says Neal. 'I'd be grateful, Anya.'

'Hang on,' says Gosling. 'Anya might not want to talk about personal stuff.'

Anya smiles.

'Thanks, Tyrone,' she says. 'But it's OK.'

Anya is proud of the things she's survived. Plus talking like this is probably helping to take her mind off the bumps in the road.

'Neal,' says Anya, 'do you know what a Sauer 38H is?'

'No,' says Neal.

Anya gives a wistful sigh.

'It's a very good gun,' she says.

We finally arrive at a town. Which, I'm relieved to see, has a railway station.

First Neal buys us all some clothes and boots.

Australians are very generous.

Most of them.

'Thanks,' I say to Neal. 'We'll pay you back.'

'Don't worry,' he says. 'My editor's good with expenses. He likes people to look well dressed in his photos. And less like they've just escaped from a children's home.'

He smiles at Anya.

'Hospitals prefer it too,' he says.

'Please thank your editor for us,' says Anya.

She seems a bit better now she's out of the car, but still very pale.

Neal takes us into a cafe and buys us a meal.

He's being so kind that I feel bad about what I have to tell him.

It was hard enough for him on the way here in the car, hearing about how Anya got pregnant. And then everything I told him about Zliv. His steering went wobbly several times.

But I have to say it.

'Neal,' I say, 'sorry, but we can't come in the car

with you to Melbourne. Anya mustn't be in a car for too long in her condition. We'll take the train instead.'

Neal stares at me. I feel terrible.

I waited till he finished eating to say it, but he still looks like he's got indigestion.

'It's only eleven hours by road,' he says. 'Less. No more than ten, probably.'

Too long, I'm tempted to say, for Anya to be stuck in a car with a person who smells like Gosling. But I don't because strangely Anya doesn't seem to have noticed.

Instead I pull my envelope out of my shirt and take out the baby book.

'It's says in here,' I tell Neal, 'that car sickness is very dangerous for a pregnant woman. I don't think we should risk it.'

I'm not sure if the book does say that. But there's another reason I don't want us to go in the car. One I don't want to tell Neal about.

'It's for the best,' I say to Neal.

Anya gives me a grateful look.

I'm glad she doesn't mind me taking over the travel arrangements.

'Which means,' I say to Neal, 'we need to borrow some money for train tickets, please.'

Neal isn't looking happy.

'Anya can stretch out on the train,' I say to him. 'So when we get to Melbourne she'll be rested and fresh for some really good newspaper photos.'

'We all will,' says Gosling.

Neal gives a sigh.

I hope he's thinking how bad it would look if his driving made a young pregnant woman sick and his editor made him write about that.

I'm also hoping he remembers that he owes us a favour. In the car I told him about Celeste's mother living somewhere in Melbourne. And how, when Celeste and Gabriek finally get to Australia, Neal will be able to write newspaper reports about two very heartwarming reunions.

If they ever get here. But I don't want to think about that now.

Neal still isn't looking happy.

'It's OK,' I say to him. 'Anya and I know how to look after ourselves.'

'So do I,' says Gosling.

'Actually,' I say to Gosling, 'why don't you go in the car with Neal? Keep him company.'

I hadn't planned to say that. It just came out.

Gosling looks hurt. Anya glares at me. Hard. I drop the idea.

'Excuse me,' I say to the waitress. 'What time is the next train to Melbourne?'

The waitress frowns and asks the man behind the counter.

'One fifteen,' says the man. 'Don't miss it. Not another one till Thursday.'

'Thanks,' I say.

I look at Neal.

'We wouldn't want to wait till Thursday,' I say.

'That would be terrible,' says Gosling.

Neal obviously agrees, because after a couple more sighs he drives us to the station.

After we've said goodbye to Neal and we're on the train and settled into a compartment and speeding across the countryside, I tell Anya the other reason I wanted us to travel on our own.

'The hospital in Melbourne,' I say. 'Do you want to risk going there?'

Anya knows what I mean.

Gosling doesn't.

'I'm sure it's a good hospital,' he says. 'One of the boys went there to have part of a plough blade removed from his leg, and he was playing cricket two months later.'

I give Gosling a look. His shoulders sag.

'Sorry,' he says. 'You're right. A baby's not part of a plough.'

'Thanks for being concerned, Tyrone,' says Anya. 'But what Felix means is that when you're my age, people take your baby and give it away.'

Gosling looks shocked. Then he sets his jaw.

'Just let them try that with yours,' he says.

We must all have been exhausted.

Halfway through talking about the hospital in Melbourne, we all started dozing off. I haven't got a clue how long we've been asleep.

I've been dreaming about Zliv.

He was just a shadowy figure in the dream, which somehow made him even scarier. My skin feels clammy and my heart is clattering faster than the train wheels.

I have to stop doing this. No point worrying about Zliv till he gets here. For now, we've got something more urgent to think about.

The hospital.

I open my eyes.

Gosling is still asleep. He's slumped with his head on Anya's shoulder. Which I think is a bit rude when you've only just met someone.

Anya is awake and doesn't look too happy about it either.

I give Gosling a nudge and he sits up, blinking.

Anya still doesn't look happy. She's frowning at me. Perhaps I was wrong. Perhaps she liked having Gosling's head on her shoulder.

I change the subject.

'Have you had any more thoughts?' I say to her. 'About the hospital in Melbourne.'

Anya doesn't say anything.

Just shakes her head.

'I reckon,' says Gosling fiercely, 'we should let that hospital know right at the start that taking and adopting is not on.'

'I feel the same,' I say. 'But what if they take the baby anyway? I don't think it's worth the risk, not even for a clean bed and some expert doctors.'

Anya doesn't seem to think it is either.

She's looking pale and her forehead is still scrunched up.

'Do you agree?' I say to her.

'I don't think we have to worry,' she says, her voice strangled with pain. 'I don't think the baby's going to wait that long. I think it's coming now.'

Maybe if you're having a baby on a crowded train, the best place is in the luggage van.

There'll probably be more space there and it'll be more private. And with a bit of luck there'll be soft bags Anya can lie on.

I go to have a look.

As I head along the corridors towards the back of the train, I see how lucky we are to have our compartment completely to ourselves. Most of the other compartments are full.

It would be very embarrassing for Anya to have strangers in our compartment. Specially now her waters have broken and the floor is flooded. The other passengers might not have a baby book and might not know why the water is there.

'Can I help you?'

That's a shame.

The luggage van isn't as private as I'd hoped. There's a guard sitting at a small table in the corner.

I'll have to switch to Plan B.

'When do we get to the next station, please?' I say to the guard, trying not to look like I'm panicking, which I am.

The guard looks at a sheet of paper.

'Twenty-eight minutes,' he says.

I hope Anya can wait that long.

'Thanks,' I say.

I go back to our compartment and tell Anya she has to hang on for twenty-eight minutes.

'Can you do it?' I say.

'How would I know?' she snaps. 'You idiot.'

I remember what the baby book says. That when women have babies, they can be a bit grumpy and short-tempered.

'I'll help her hang on,' says Gosling.

Strangely Anya doesn't call him an idiot.

I fetch some drinking water from the corridor for Anya, then go back to the luggage van to get started with Plan B.

Which is to distract the guard so that when we get to the next station, Gosling can help Anya off the train without the guard seeing. We don't want him spotting her labour pains and calling an ambulance.

I start off by pretending I need to check the name of the next station.

The guard looks a bit irritated, but tells me.

I tell him about Polish station names for a while, but I can see he's losing interest.

'Do you have any children?' I say to him.

He looks surprised.

'Four,' he says.

'Can I ask you a question about them?' I say.

'S'pose,' he says.

'When they were born,' I say, 'did the doctor seal the end of the umbilical cord using heat or a suture?'

'We're in luck,' says Gosling.

After the train has chugged away, we come out from our hiding place behind the waiting room and look around at the deserted station.

Gosling's right, we are.

We're in luck that the guard was so interested in my baby book. Mostly because each time one of his was born, he was in the pub.

We're also in luck that Gosling got Anya off the train without the guard seeing. Plus he brought the cushions from two seats, the water bottle that's usually chained up in the corridor, and the metal hand-washing bowl from next to the train toilet. Also without the guard seeing.

The train driver and the assistant train driver didn't see either. This station is mostly a water stop for the engine, and they were busy with the hose from the big tank on the platform.

Which was also lucky.

What's less lucky is that the waiting-room door is locked.

'I need to lie down,' groans Anya.

Gosling and I arrange the seat cushions on the platform so Anya can stretch out on them.

She doesn't do much stretching out.

She huddles on her side, knees against her chest, panting painfully.

I kneel next to her and stroke her hair.

'Anya,' I say gently. 'If there's anything we can do to help you with the pain of the contractions, just say so, OK?'

Anya looks up at me with her big dark eyes.

'Shut up,' she snarls.

The baby book didn't make it clear that women in labour could be this grumpy.

I hear thunder in the distance and glance at the sky. Rain clouds are building up. We need to get Anya inside.

Gosling must be thinking the same thing. He's inspecting the padlock on the waiting-room door.

'I've still got the toothpick,' he says to Anya.

I wait for her to snarl at him.

'Thank you, Tyrone,' she says.

At least it's dry in here.

Outside, the rain is lashing across the platform and the wind is howling in the dusk almost as loudly as Anya.

I wish there was more I could do for her.

All the medical books I've carefully read, all the medical information I've tried hard to remember, all the knowledge I've studied about how the human body works, and it turns out that the human body knows how it works all on its own.

Anya arches her back on the cushions as a big contraction makes her gasp and yell and screech.

I wipe her wet face with the sleeve that Gosling kindly tore off my shirt.

He gives her sips from the water bottle.

The contractions are every couple of minutes now. The baby book says that means not long to go.

'Not long to go,' I say to Anya.

'Get lost,' she grunts.

After the next contraction passes, Anya leaves her knees raised and pulls her skirt further up and puts her hand between her legs.

'Don't look,' she moans.

'We're not looking,' I say. 'We're helping.'

'Oh my God,' says Gosling. 'Look at that.'

I look. The top of the baby's head is appearing.

'Breathe,' I say to Anya and I do it myself, big regular panting breaths to remind her what to do between pushes.

Another contraction.

Anya bares her teeth and stops breathing and her face bulges with the pushing.

More of the baby's head comes out.

I put my hands down there, ready.

Anya drags a huge groaning gasp of air into herself and pushes again and suddenly the baby tumbles out in a gush, wet and wriggling and alive.

It's not dry in here any more.

There's blood on the floor.

Anya's face and hair are sodden with sweat.

And as I put the tiny slippery person into Anya's arms, we're all crying, all of us, because ever since we were born the world has been boiling over with bad things and now we've got a thing that is wonderful and precious and really really good.

Maybe the pawn shop.

Or would the dentist be better?

No, I think the pawn shop, because there doesn't seem to be a dentist anywhere along this deserted dusty main street.

That's the problem with trying to sell gold in a very small Australian country town. No dentist.

I check my clothes for streaks of dirt and visible bloodstains, and go into the pawn shop.

The man behind the counter wakes up and looks at me suspiciously.

'Hello,' I say. 'Can you please tell me how much this is worth?'

I put Cyryl's ring on the counter.

The man rubs his ginger hair and does a few more suspicious looks at me and at least a couple at the ring.

I notice his looks are getting a bit less suspicious and a bit more greedy.

This is probably because I forgot to brush my hair and I've got cobwebs in it from sleeping on the waiting-room floor and he thinks I'm desperate.

Which I am.

'You're not from around here,' says the man.

'Just passing through,' I say.

'Ah,' says the man. 'Fruit-picking family. Season's almost over, so you'll be gone soon.'

I don't tell him he's wrong, because he's right about the last bit. We'll be gone as soon as Anya feels ready to go.

'Where's it from?' says the man.

'Poland,' I say.

'May I?' he says.

He picks up the ring, examines it, weighs it, taps it, puts a drop of liquid onto it, and does some other things to it.

'It's solid gold,' I say.

'I know,' says the man.

'How much is it worth?' I say.

'Fifty pounds,' says the man. 'Or two pounds if it's stolen.'

'It's stolen,' I say. 'I'll take the two pounds.'

When I get back to the waiting room, my arms are aching from all the things I'm carrying.

The ache disappears as soon as I step inside and see Anya sitting on the cushions with her tiny daughter. Who is sucking Anya's milk, just like the baby book says she would.

I put my load down and stand there, grinning.

Anya grins back at me.

'Hooray,' says Gosling, who's crouching next to them. 'What did you get?'

Gosling has filled the bowl with water and is wringing out the torn-off sleeve of my shirt. Judging by the pink colour of the liquid, he's been helping Anya clean up.

I think he's getting over his fear of cold water, which is good.

'Bread and cheese,' I say. 'And milk and fruit and carrots and nappies. And blankets from the pawn shop. And soap and disinfectant and a sharp knife for the clean and heat.'

There's more, but I stop and stare.

It doesn't look like a clean and heat will be needed. The umbilical cord attached to the baby's tummy has disappeared.

Anya sees me looking.

'Tyrone did it,' she says. 'He bit it off.'

I go over and have a look at the baby's tummy, slowly, so I don't seem bossy.

It's a good bite. The little stump that will be the baby's belly button looks clean and neat. Bit of disinfectant and it'll be fine.

'Tyrone was very kind,' says Anya. 'He went outside and buried the cord and the placenta.'

She gives Gosling a grateful look.

'And see,' she says, 'He's made us curtains. He stuck them up with tree sap.'

All over the windows of the waiting room are sheets of old newspaper.

'There's only four trains a week,' says Gosling. 'Two in each direction. Monday and Thursday. So if we keep the door locked and stay quiet, I think we'll be right.'

I give him a grateful nod.

I should say something, but I need a moment to get used to Gosling being such a housekeeping and train-timetable expert.

'You're very kind too, Felix,' says Anya. 'Getting us all these things.'

'There's no rush to go,' I say. 'Take your time and get strong and we'll head off to Melbourne in a few days when you're ready.'

Anya gives me one of her grateful looks.

I don't want her and Gosling seeing me blushing, so I say something to distract them.

'I called Neal from a public phone,' I tell them. 'He panicked a bit at first when he heard we aren't in a hospital. But when I told him we're in a place specially designed for people to rest in, he calmed down. He said he'll be waiting for us in Melbourne when we get there.'

'You're amazing,' says Gosling.

'We're very grateful,' says Anya, stroking the baby's head. 'Me and Ruby.'

I smile. It's a nice name.

Anya pats the floor.

I sit down next to them.

Anya holds Ruby out to me and I take her.

I cradle her in my arms, one of the most precious things I've ever held.

I can't help feeling sad all of a sudden, thinking about other precious people I've held in my arms. I held them as close as I could, really close, but I still lost them.

Sunlight is filtering in through the newspaper curtains, making the big headlines stand out in silhouette.

WAR OVER

FIGHTING ENDS

PEACE

I gaze at them.

Old newspapers, about the past.

But I hope they're telling us something about the future too.

'Neal,' I yell into the phone. 'Calm down.'

I don't know if swearing on the telephone is illegal in Australia. If it is, Neal's in big trouble.

'You're right,' I say to him. 'Our stay is turning out to be longer than I said. But Anya isn't ready, so we'll get the train on Monday. We'll be arriving in Melbourne at the same time as we would have done a week ago.'

Neal says we'd better.

Which is the first thing he's said this morning that a nun wouldn't mind hearing.

Speaking of nuns . . .

'Neal,' I say, lowering my voice even though the post office is deserted. 'Any problem about me and Anya escaping from the children's homes?'

'Nothing,' says Neal. 'I think the authorities want to keep it under wraps. I'm trying to find out what's going on.'

There's one more thing I need to ask him.

'Any news about Mrs Prejenka?' I say.

'I've found her,' says Neal. 'She works in a pub in South Melbourne.'

For a moment I can't speak. I think about how Celeste will feel when she hears.

'Does Celeste know?' I say.

'I sent her a telegram today,' says Neal.

We say goodbye.

I don't ask him if he's heard anything about Zliv. Sometimes a piece of news is so good, you don't want to spoil it with something bad.

Why do trains make you sleepy?

We've all been dozing on this one too.

I'm not complaining. Sometimes sleep is what you need to get away from your problems for a while. Specially problems that don't involve your neck possibly being broken, just your heart.

Anya is still asleep, her face peaceful, her head on Gosling's shoulder. She's been doing that a lot over the last few days. I don't blame her. Gosling's shoulder is almost as big as a pillow.

But I could put a pillow on my shoulder if she wanted me to.

Gosling is awake, with Ruby tucked in the crook of his big arm. He's very gentle with her, which he should be, all the practice he gets looking after her.

'Hello, Ruby,' I whisper, smiling at her.

Anya opens her eyes and smiles too.

'Ruby was my mother's name,' says Gosling, with a fond look at Anya. 'I'm very honoured.'

I struggle to keep the smile on my face.

I don't manage to. I've got a mother as well, and she's also dead.

But it's not just hearing about Ruby's name that's making me feel jealous.

I've noticed something else.

Gosling and Anya are doing it again.

Holding hands.

They've been doing it for the last couple of days. When they thought I wasn't watching. Now they're doing it out in the open.

Anya is watching me.

'Tyrone,' she says. 'Could you get more water from the corridor, please?'

'Of course,' says Gosling, giving Ruby to Anya and grabbing our water bottle and going outside.

Anya looks at me and pats the cushion where Gosling was just sitting.

I go and sit next to her.

She puts Ruby into my arms.

When I look up from Ruby's dear little face,

from the bubbles of saliva on her tiny lips, Anya is gazing at me.

It's a fond gaze, and a sad one.

'Felix,' she says. 'You're my best friend and I love you. But we can't always choose what happens.'

We look at each other for a long time.

'You're right,' I say quietly. 'We can't.'

She is right.

In a few hours we'll arrive in Melbourne.

Our hope is that Anya will be able to keep Ruby, and I'll be able to get Gabriek and Celeste to Australia, and the Australian police will be able to handle something very scary if it comes along.

But we don't know what will happen.

We can only hope.

Over the next few days and weeks, life will let us know if it plans to be good or bad.

Maybe Neal isn't allowed onto the platform without a ticket. Maybe he's waiting for us on the other side of the barrier.

'Hey,' says the ticket inspector at the barrier gate. 'These tickets are a week old.'

'Sorry,' I say. 'We had to break the journey. The baby. You know what it's like.'

I hope he does. I can see faint dribble stains on his shoulder, but they might be his.

The inspector looks sternly at Anya and Ruby.

Ruby gurgles at him and Anya smiles wearily.

'If you're going to arrest anybody,' says Gosling, 'arrest me. If you have to.'

The inspector looks tempted, but waves us all through. And there, on the other side of the barrier, is Neal.

'Hello,' he says.

Then he stops and stares.

'This is Ruby,' I say.

'Hello, Ruby,' says Neal.

I could tell on the phone how worried he was about Anya and Ruby. I told him to concentrate on the good things, but he wouldn't listen.

He looks very relieved.

'Congratulations, Anya,' says Neal. 'People will be very happy to meet you and little Ruby.'

A smiling woman with grey hair steps forward, shakes Anya's hand, then Gosling's, then mine.

'Wonderful to meet you,' she says in Polish.

'Mrs Prejenka,' I say.

Sometimes you can be a different height, shape and age, and still look just like somebody else.

'I've heard lots about you all,' says Mrs Prejenka. 'Or rather I've read lots.'

She holds up several copies of a newspaper.

She said that last bit in English. I think it was so Neal could understand. The newspaper must be the one he works for.

I reach inside my shirt for my envelope with Celeste's letter in it.

'You must all be parched,' says Neal. 'Let's have a cup of tea. We've got lots to catch up on.'

'And then afterwards,' says Mrs Prejenka, 'you will all come to my house. For a rest.' She looks at Gosling. 'And a bath. It's not a big house, but I hope you will all stay for as long as you like.'

We all thank her very much. After a week on a hard waiting-room floor, an actual house sounds wonderful.

Neal's right, we are all parched, so I like the idea of a cup of tea as well.

What I'm not so keen on is the nervous glance Neal gives me as we head to the station cafe. As if there's something he's worried about telling me.

Mrs Prejenka slowly lowers Celeste's letter onto the cafe table and looks at us with tears in her eyes.

'Neal told me my daughter is alive,' she says. 'But now I really know.'

'Celeste wants to see you very much,' I say.

Mrs Prejenka leans over and kisses me on the cheek.

'Thank you, Felix,' she whispers.

'I sent Celeste a telegram yesterday,' says Neal. 'Care of Flight Lieutenant Wagstaff at the air base in Poland. I gave her my newspaper's phone number and told her she can call reverse charge.'

Mrs Prejenka's eyes are shining.

'Thank you,' she says.

'As her mother,' says Neal, 'you should be the one to tell her the good news. That she'll be here as soon as the migrant boats start sailing.'

I stare at Neal.

That must mean Gabriek as well.

'It's not official yet,' says Neal to Mrs Prejenka. 'But the Australian government are planning a new policy. They want to increase our population. Bring in lots of people to help build the Australia of the future. Skilled people like Celeste.'

211

'And Gabriek,' I say.

'If he's the person who brought you up,' says Neal, giving me a grin, 'I'd say he's very skilled.'

Neal hands me one of the newspapers that Mrs Prejenka was holding. It's folded to a page with a big article on it. In the middle of the article is the photo from the local paper of me and Gosling in our cricket shirts.

'We published this a few days ago,' says Neal.

'Read it,' says Anya. 'It's brilliant.'

She and Gosling are reading it in one of Mrs Prejenka's other copies. While I was listening to Neal, I could hear Gosling helping Anya with some of the English words.

I study the article.

Neal has written about everything me and Anya told him. Our war experiences and our trip out here and my dream of studying medicine at Melbourne University and everything.

'I thought the Australian government wanted to keep the plane crash secret,' I say to Neal.

'They did,' he says. 'But my editor decided to print the details whether they liked it or not. So the government has decided there's a positive side to the story. And that positive side, Felix, is you.'

'Me?' I say.

'Felix Salinger, the first post-war migrant to Australia,' says Neal. 'Leading the way for the thousands who'll follow. Showing the Australian people what a good idea it'll be.'

I'm stunned.

As it sinks in, I'm also a bit worried about Anya feeling left out.

I glance at her.

She gives me a look across little Ruby's head. One of the grateful ones that still make me blush, but not quite as much.

I'm going to be a bit busy, her look says. Would you mind doing it?

I'm so lucky to have her as a friend.

'Tomorrow, Felix,' says Neal, 'we're doing a special photo shoot. In the Faculty of Medicine at Melbourne University. My editor wants a follow-up article about your plans to be a doctor. With lots of photos.'

Neal pauses, and I can see there's definitely something he's nervous about telling me.

'In particular,' says Neal, 'he wants photos of you at a lecture with medical students. With lots of real medical science on display. There might be body parts. Could you cope with that?'

Gosling splutters with laughter.

'Felix can cope alright,' he says. 'You should see him dissect a pig.'

What I'm not coping with so well is that after Neal tops up everyone's tea, he takes me off to show me a special locomotive.

I'm not really interested in locomotives. I'm more interested that Neal has got that expression on his face again, as if there's something else he's worried about telling me.

He hands me a small piece torn from the page of a newspaper.

'We printed this yesterday,' he says.

It's just a few paragraphs and it looks like it's from the bottom of a page.

I read it.

It's about how a guard at a military air base near Sydney was found a couple of days ago with his throat cut.

I read it a few more times, then fold it up and give it back to Neal.

'It might be nothing,' says Neal. 'But just to be safe, I tried to contact that Mr Chase and Mr Petrie you told me about. Hard fellas to get onto. So I left a message. Haven't heard back.'

'It probably is nothing,' I say, feeling sick.

'A coincidence,' says Neal.

'Absolutely,' I say.

I tell myself to stop being silly.

Military guards must get into fights all the time. Squabbling over money or alcohol or girlfriends or cricket. And they probably prefer to fight with knives rather than guns so the senior officers don't hear them.

Anyway, Sydney is hundreds of miles away.

'You OK, Felix?' says Neal.

I nod.

I don't say anything else because sometimes, as

Gabriek taught me, you have to concentrate on the most important thing.

And I don't want Neal worrying and cancelling the photo shoot tomorrow. I want to be in lots of photos for the Australian government, to make sure Gabriek and Celeste get a place on the first available boat.

Plenty of time after that to worry.

Maybe the stress of this will give me a heart attack. Maybe they'll end up doing the university medical lecture about me.

It's my fault.

I should have said something to Neal yesterday. That I was worried sick when I read the newspaper report about the dead guard with the slit throat.

The minute we arrived here at the university this morning, I regretted I hadn't.

As soon as the staff told us the news.

'A man,' said one of the secretaries. 'We didn't know who he was. Hanging around the Faculty Of Medicine yesterday asking about a Polish boy called Felix Salinger.'

'Did he have an accent?' I said.

Another secretary nodded.

I felt sick again.

Neal looked a bit pale too.

'Cripes,' he muttered.

It's torture, waiting in this small room while Neal's off trying to find out more. I've told him how dangerous Zliv is, but I don't know if he really understands. Luckily there'll be government people here this morning for the photo shoot, but still.

Someone knocks on the door.

My internal organs twitch.

Neal comes in.

'Couldn't find out any more about the bloke,' he says. 'But I reckon I know who it is. I should have twigged before, when they said accent. There's a journalist, Irish mongrel, chief political reporter at the Herald, always trying to muscle in on my stories. When I get my hands on him, I'll kill him.'

I stare at Neal, taking this in.

When a man with an honest face tells you something that's very likely true, you'd be foolish not to believe him.

I think that's what Gabriek would say.

'Thank you,' I say. 'I feel much better.'

'So if he pops up again,' says Neal, 'I don't want you saying a word to him, right?'

'Right,' I say.

Maybe I'll faint.

Maybe just stepping onto the stage of this huge lecture theatre will make me pass out.

Not because of the jars of body parts on the shelves. Not because of the gleaming operating table in the middle of the stage. Not even because of the dead body lying on the table, all marked up for study and dissection.

What I'm worried about are the live people.

Lots of them in rows and rows of seats, stretching away so far I can hardly see the ones at the back. Students, mostly, who'll soon be wondering why a kid is showing off on stage when he didn't even go to high school.

Anya and Ruby and Gosling and Mrs Prejenka are up the back somewhere. So, Neal reckons, are a few people from the Australian government. But as I peek in through this door at the side of the stage, I can't see any of them, not even with my glasses polished.

'OK, Felix?' says Neal, slapping me on the shoulder.

I nod, not speaking in case my voice wobbles.

'The photographer's here,' says Neal. 'We're just waiting for the professor who's going to make an entrance with you. It'll be a great photo.'

Neal glances at his watch.

'I'd better go and make sure the prof's on his way,' he says. 'Wait here. I'll be back.'

He's gone before I can ask him if professors of medicine have pills to calm wobbly tummies.

I try to do some deep breaths.

It's what Gabriek taught me to do when I was living in a hole under his barn and I'd hear people arrive at the farm who might be Nazis.

Deep breaths.

While you do it, you have to think only about your breathing.

'Australian boy,' hisses a voice.

Hard to think about breathing when a clown like Gosling sneaks up behind you and grabs you. He probably thinks this mucking around is helping me relax.

Idiot.

'At last,' hisses a wet voice.

A cruel voice.

Speaking Polish, which Gosling doesn't.

I freeze.

Then I do the technique that Yuli taught me. The one that gets you away from somebody who's got their arm round your throat.

But Zliv's skinny arm is like steel rope.

I try something else. I kick one heel up into where I think his private part will be.

It is.

His arm slips and I'm under it, crashing hard through the door into the lecture theatre.

Neal didn't tell me about the step.

I trip and fall flat.

The rows of students are staring, stunned, and then they start yelling. This tells me that Zliv has come through the door.

I roll to one side, hoping he'll miss with his first lunge and I'll have a chance to grab a weapon from the shelf like a scalpel or a jar of brains.

But he doesn't miss.

His hand feels like a steel claw as it lifts me off the floor.

His arm clamps round my throat again, this time with the glint of a knife in his other hand as he drags me backwards out through the doorway.

The last thing I see before the door swings shut is the body on the operating table, its head lolling, a pink incision line across its throat.

'Normally,' hisses Zliv into my ear, 'you would be dead already. But this is for my brother. So we do it slowly.'

It's hard for me to see what he's doing now because my glasses have just fallen off and his arm is so tight round my neck my eyes are seeing light only in bubbles.

I hear something scraping.

I manage a glimpse over my shoulder.

We're in front of a lift. Zliv is sliding the criss-cross metal doors open. He must want to take me up onto the roof or somewhere private like that so he can do his dissection without any professors watching.

I hear people bursting out of the lecture theatre.

Zliv throws me inside the lift. My head bashes on the floor. I hear him pulling the lift doors shut.

Then I hear another sound.

The safety catch being released on a gun.

'Come out,' yells a voice.

I see Zliv reach into his pocket with the hand that's not holding the knife.

I roll into a corner.

A gun goes off.

Zliv slams into the back wall of the lift.

Through the lattice metalwork of the lift doors, I try to catch a glimpse of the person outside.

Not Anya, surely?

No, a man. One I've seen before. In a familiar dark government suit.

Mr Chase.

The lift isn't going up. Zliv starts to slide down, leaving a slime of red on the lift wall. He lunges forward, grabbing at the brass handle on the lift control box to stop himself hitting the floor.

Both his hands slam onto the handle and for a few seconds he hangs there.

The lift starts to go up.

With a tortured screech, the weight of Zliv's body tears the control box off the wall, wires sparking.

The lift stops.

Zliv crashes to the floor.

The doors don't open. I can see through the lattice that we're between floors. I pull the control box from under Zliv's body and frantically work the handle but nothing happens.

The lift is stuck.

I can hear muffled voices shouting above and below. And another sound. Much closer.

Zliv's wet breathing. Like a milkshake being sucked up a straw.

I scramble to my feet.

My first thought is to get away from him. My next thought is to grab his knife or his gun and make sure he never kills another innocent person.

But then I stop.

He's lying on his side, his breath bubbling, no other part of him moving. I've been around a lot of unconscious people, and he's the most unconscious I've ever seen.

Carefully I roll him onto his back.

The wound in his chest is huge. Ribbons of flesh mixed up with ribbons of cloth. Lots of meat showing. Broken blood vessels spewing blood.

I hesitate, but only for a second.

His fingers, I see, are yellow from cigarettes.

I feel in his pockets until I find his cigarette lighter. I grab his knife from the floor and do a heat. No time for clean. As soon as I have heat, I seal the first pumping blood vessel in a stenching cloud of sour smoke.

More heat.

Another cloud.

I'm not doing this fast enough. I'm kneeling in blood and more is spewing out.

Heat.

Smoke.

Heat.

Smoke.

He coughs blood over the lighter, a throatful of it, and I feel for his pulse while I'm waiting for the lighter to spark again.

I'm still feeling for his pulse when the lift gives a big jolt and the doors open and hands grab me.

I start sobbing, but I don't stop feeling for the pulse even after I realise there isn't one any more.

Because you don't.

Not in this job.

Maybe today Mrs Prejenka will stop looking at me as if I'm her son and she's my very proud mother.

No, I don't think she will.

'Felix,' she says. 'Let me cook you another egg.'

'Thanks, Mrs Prejenka,' I say. 'But I've had two already. I'll use up all your rations.'

'Aurelina,' says Mrs Prejenka sternly. 'My name's Aurelina.'

Ruby does a loud burp on my shoulder, which gives me a good excuse not to try and say Mrs Prejenka's name and get it wrong again.

'I have plenty of eggs,' she says. 'What have I told you? You get eggs if you work in a pub.'

What she told me was, you get eggs if you work in a pub and give people drinks after the six o'clock closing time.

'When Celeste and Gabriek get here on the boat,' says Mrs Prejenka, 'they should work in a pub.'

I smile. I'm pretty sure Gabriek will have other career plans.

Ruby does another burp.

Gently I wipe milk off her chin with her bib.

Mrs Prejenka sighs happily.

She picks up the tattered newspaper from the kitchen table and tenderly brushes the crumbs off. I think she loves this newspaper article even more than the first one.

'I showed this to the boys in the pub,' she says. 'They want to give you eggs too. When Anya and Tyrone get back from their walk in the park, we'll go to the pub.'

I smile again.

'When they get back,' I say, 'we've got to study. High school starts next week.'

'To be a good student,' says Mrs Prejenka, 'you need eggs.'

She kisses me gently on the forehead and taps her finger on the newspaper.

'*We hope to see him back here in a few years,*' she says, quoting her favourite bit, '*said the Dean of the Faculty of Medicine.*'

'He was just being kind,' I say.

'He was being sensible,' says Mrs Prejenka. 'He knows what you did in that lift.'

I sigh.

I know what she's going to say next, and part of me thinks she should stop saying it, but the truth is I don't want her to stop.

'In that lift,' she says, 'you were a doctor.'

Ruby does a big burp and I can feel warm baby milk running down inside my collar. Which is a useful thing when you might be getting a bit ahead of yourself.

Mrs Prejenka hurries out to get a clean bib.

I lift Ruby off my shoulder and hold her to my chest.

I look down at her angel face, which has never known things that are bad, and for a moment it feels like I haven't either.

I have of course.

But when I think about the future, things feel good.

Very good.

Even very very good.

Maybe.

Dear Reader

My plan is that one day there will be seven in Felix's family of books and then my work with him will be done.

Maybe *brings the total so far to six. It joins* Once, Then, After *and* Soon *in exploring Felix's early years as he struggles to keep his friends and optimism alive through World War Two and what follows.*

Between writing Then *and* After, *I wanted to find out how the experiences of Felix's youth, in particular the terrible years of the Holocaust, would shape his adult life. So I wrote* Now, *in which the 80-year-old Felix, still battling and still optimistic, revisits his early years in an unexpected and life-changing way.*

The seventh book, Always, *which I plan to write in the next couple of years, will bring Felix's story full circle. Felix will have the opportunity for an act of courage and generosity bigger than anything he's attempted before. A final chance, perilous but irresistible, to say thank you to the many special people in his life.*

There are two reasons I call this a family of books. The first is that years ago, when I started my work with Felix, I quickly came to see him and his friends and the brave adults who look after them as just that, a family.

The other reason I hesitate to call these books a series is that I've tried to write them so they can be read in any order. Most of us prefer reading to waiting, and sometimes we can't choose exactly when we get our hands on a particular book.

If Maybe *is your first encounter with Felix, please don't be perturbed. After reading it you'll know a few* things about his earlier years, but not enough to spoil the other stories.

Thank you Kathy Toohey for the research advice. For the publishing, editing, design, marketing and distribution of Maybe, my heartfelt thanks to Laura Harris, Heather Curdie, Helen Levene, Tony Palmer, Dorothy Tonkin, Tina Gumnior and Kristin Gill. And my warm appreciation to everyone else at Penguin Random House in Australia and the UK, and to many teams at publishing houses in other countries, all of whose skill and dedication help Felix on his journey into the hands and hearts of readers.

Felix's stories come from my imagination, but also from a period of history that was all too real. I couldn't have written any of these stories without first reading many books about the Holocaust and what came after. Books that are full of the real voices of the people who lived and struggled and loved and faced death in that terrible time.

You can find details of some of my research reading on my website. I hope you get to delve into some of those books and help keep alive the memory of those people.

This story is my imagination trying to grasp the unimaginable.

Their stories are the real stories.

Morris Gleitzman
May 2017
www.morrisgleitzman.com

MORRIS GLEITZMAN

Everybody
deserves
to have
something good in their life.

At least

Once.

Once I escaped from an orphanage to find Mum and Dad.
Once I saved a girl called Zelda from a burning house.
Once I made a Nazi with toothache laugh.
My name is Felix.
This is my story.

'... moving, haunting and funny in almost equal measure,
and always gripping...' *Guardian*

'This is one of the most profoundly moving novels
I have ever read. Gleitzman at his very best has created one
of the most tender, endearing characters ever to grace the
pages of a book.' *Sunday Tasmanian*

'... a story of courage, survival and friendship told
with humour from a child's view of the world.'
West Australian

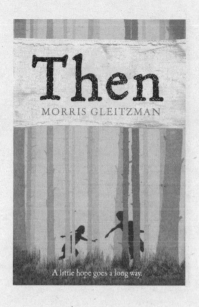

I had a plan for me and Zelda.
Pretend to be someone else.
Find new parents.
Be safe for ever.
Then the Nazis came.

' . . . an exquisitely told, unflinching and courageous novel.'
Age

'[Gleitzman] has accomplished something extraordinary,
presenting the best and the worst of humanity without stripping
his characters of dignity or his readers of hope.'
Guardian

'Gleitzman's Felix and Zelda are two of the finest and
sure-to-endure characters created in recent times.'
Hobart Mercury

After the Nazis took my parents I was scared.
After they killed my best friend I was angry.
After they ruined my thirteenth birthday I was determined.
To get to the forest.
To join forces with Gabriek and Yuli.
To be a family.
To defeat the Nazis after all.

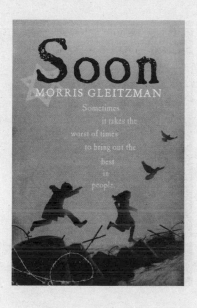

I hoped that soon the Nazis would be defeated.
And they were.
I hoped that soon the war would be over.
And it was.
I hoped that soon we would be safe.
But we aren't.

'An amazing story . . . it is Felix's indomitable optimism that shines
through . . . making us believe that trust, goodness and love will prevail.'
Magpies

' . . . an awesomely epic adventure . . . It is the best book I have ever read!'
Guardian, young reviewer

' . . . unexpectedly beautiful in its balance of hope and despair.'
Mostly Books

BOOK OF THE YEAR – YOUNGER READERS
CHILDREN'S BOOK COUNCIL OF AUSTRALIA AWARDS

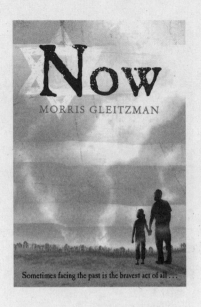

Now

MORRIS GLEITZMAN

Sometimes facing the past is the bravest act of all . . .

Once I didn't know about my grandfather Felix's scary childhood.
Then I found out what the Nazis did to his best friend Zelda.
Now I understand why Felix does the things he does.
At least he's got me.
My name is Zelda too.
This is our story.

'*Now* is an edifying and tender, nuanced novel from
an exceptionally compassionate author.'
Age

'Gleitzman has a special way of seeing the world through the eyes
of a child, and generations of readers are grateful to him for it.'
West Australian

'Gleitzman's trademark fine balance of tragedy and
comedy is as sure as ever.'
Guardian